Tom Tomaszewski works as a psychotherapist specialising in addiction at a private clinic, Charter, in central London. He was born in 1966 and grew up in South London, spending large amounts of time in the Scottish Highlands. His mother, a nurse who worked with the Romany population of St Mary Cray in Bromley, introduced him to books and music alongside medicine and psychology, all of which continue to interest him. His father, a printing engineer, came from a family of dissenting Polish patriots. His aunt died in Auschwitz and his grandfather was regularly prosecuted for an anti-Prussian column he wrote called *Polish Fire*.

www.tomtomaszewski.com

First published in 2016
by Dodo Ink, an imprint of
Dodo Publishing Co Ltd
Flat 5, 21 Silverlands, Buxton SK17 6QH
www.dodoink.com

The right of Tom Tomaszewski to be identified as the author
of this work has been asserted in accordance with Section 77
of the Copyright, Designs and Patents Act 1988

A CIP record for this book is available from the British Library

Cover design: Carolina Rodriguez Fuenmayor (artwork)
James Nunn (typography)
Copy-editor: Jayne White
Proofreaders: Dan Coxon and Tomoé Hill
Typesetter: Ben Ottridge

ISBN 978-0-9935758-2-2 paperback

Printed and bound in Great Britain by TJ International
Trecerus Industrial Estate, Padstow, Cornwall PL28 8RW.

THE ELEVENTH LETTER

TOM TOMASZEWSKI

Dodo Ink would like to give special
thanks to Stephen Wright

For Sarah

... what haunts are not the dead, but the gaps left within us by the secrets of others.

Nicolas Abraham

PROLOGUE
PISA, 1986

After a few moments I heard myself speaking.

'My name's Christopher Katiwa.' I sounded so much younger. That was August 1986. I was listening to a tape recording from nearly twenty-five years ago – in my study, cut off from the world by snow.

Louise replied. 'Doctor *Kateeva*. I wondered how you pronounced it.'

'Chris.'

And I remembered how she looked, sitting opposite me in that strange, shadowy, cluttered room at the police building in Pisa. I remembered her blue eyes, then her heart-shaped face and her dark hair; her arms, folded in her lap, and her legs, which were crossed, and her black shoes with their sharp heels. She sat opposite me, on the verge of a smile, a few strands of hair across her face. I noticed the smell of her perfume, which was something musky and European, not at all English, and the way her skirt folded over her knee. I remembered the suit she was wearing, probably Chanel, and the way it fitted perfectly, the jacket unbuttoned, and her silver-grey shirt.

'My blood hurts.'

'Your blood hurts?'

'Yes.'

What could I say?

'I don't see why I have to go through everything again.' The smile, whatever there'd been of it, was gone and she looked tired.

'You don't have to.'

She closed her eyes and opened them slowly. I imagined her counting to ten. 'Simon said that.'

I nodded.

She looked at her hands, slowly moving her fingers. 'He was good at saying nothing, too.'

'But you spoke to him.'

She stared at me. 'Did you say *Chris*?' She waited, as if she wanted to see what I'd do.

I felt my skin prickle. 'Yes, Chris.' She was moving at a different pace from me.

'*Chris*.' She said it with an Italian accent. 'Are you Italian?'

I told her I was English.

'Chris.' She looked surprised and glanced towards the window. 'Chris. How funny, I could have sworn there's something foreign about you. What's going on with your name?'

'My father was Polish.'

She stretched her arms in front of her, clasping then letting go of her wrists, extending her fingers. 'I knew it.' She relaxed, letting her arms fall. 'Can you get me out of here?' She looked away before I could reply. 'No ... How old are you? You look very young.'

'Thirty,' I said. I remembered, as I listened to the tape, how young I had felt.

'Are you experienced?'

I was young, but she couldn't have been much older than me. I'd just finished my training and I wasn't about to get into that. Simon was older and more confident, with a reputation. He had no idea that I'd gone behind his back – gone to Pisa. He was on holiday, his job done, somewhere on the other side of the world.

'I want to help you.'

She laughed. 'Simon didn't go *that* far.'

'No?'

'No. He gave me the impression I was beyond help. He thinks I killed Kate, doesn't he? He thinks I killed John.'

I didn't reply. Silence, I thought. Silence was better. She waved her hand, as if she was used to it.

'My solicitor told me that's what he thinks.'

She shrugged, closed her eyes, tapped her foot, and opened her eyes again, wide, inviting me to look into them. 'You're still here?'

'Your solicitor asked me to speak to you.'

'So?'

'I asked him not to say anything to you before I saw you.'

'Because?'

'I didn't want you to know I was coming in case something got in the way.' I hesitated with what I was about to say. 'I don't think you killed anybody.'

She smiled.

'I don't know what happened, but I don't think you're a killer.'

She shrugged again. 'I didn't.' She paused and glanced at me as if we were sharing a joke. 'What makes you think I didn't?'

I shifted. She raised her eyebrows enough to let me know she'd noticed.

'I don't know.'

She looked at the floor. 'You don't know.' It felt as if she was slipping away.

'No. I don't.' The space between us was unravelling, the tension slackening.

'Why not?'

I told her: 'Your story sounds like a ghost story.'

More distance, as if the ground between us was going to open up. Nothing would cover it. 'Do you believe in ghosts?'

'No.'

'Neither do I,' she said.

'Then why did it sound as if you were telling Simon a ghost story?'

'It's how it happened.' She went over to the window and looked down onto the police vehicles in the courtyard, their roof-lights glittering in the sun. There was something in that look, a kind of intention, which I couldn't work out.

I looked around me, at the piles of old police files and junk stacked along the walls: newspaper, two pairs of boots, a cardboard box, a painting of a white cat with elaborate whiskers. We were talking somewhere that had once been the dining room of a Renaissance villa. Now it was paintingless, chandelierless, tableless ...

If I glanced at all that stuff around us then back at Louise, it felt as if I only had to blink and all the old furniture would fall back into place. The junk would be gone. The trailing cable hanging from the ceiling with its two bare leads, nasty-looking strands of copper wire, would grow a glass chandelier with candles.

'I thought about lying,' she said. 'Some of the things I said to Simon, if I said them again, I'd say them differently. But I didn't lie.'

'You were in Florence.'

'I was working. It was planned weeks before. I went there after the wedding at Wasing.'

'But you were in Florence, what, a couple of hours away?'

'I spent all of my time in the library there – right until the moment Kate called me. Then I went to see her. And yes, it only took a couple of hours.'

I replied quietly. 'I need to be completely clear with you. If you keep saying what you're saying, then they'll find you guilty.'

She stared at me long enough for us to grow old, die, be buried, or burned, cast away, dust. My mind was drifting – I brought myself back.

'Do you want me to start lying?'

'Talk to me.'

'Really?'

'See what happens.'

'See what happens?'

'Will you think about it?'

'Perhaps,' she replied. 'Not now, though.'

'Will you see me again?'

'Tomorrow,' she said. 'Now go away.' She wasn't even looking at me.

I nodded, hesitated, then rang the little bell, a cowbell on a leather strap: a strange arrangement I'd been presented with to call the guard outside the room when I wanted to leave.

'That thing's ridiculous,' she said. 'That bell.'

It was. I ended our first interview with a cowbell.

CHAPTER 1
HARLEY STREET, 2010

That was the tape – part of it. This is how I ended up listening to it.

It was late in the afternoon. I was standing in my consulting room, surrounded by half-empty boxes, staring out of the window onto Harley Street and watching the snow fall. I was supposed to be packing up to move, but I wasn't making much progress. What should I take with me, what should I take home, and what should I dispose of?

I noticed a mark in the mist on the glass. A line. A letter L; a mark I must have made. L for – what had I been thinking of? I couldn't remember.

My handwriting was sometimes almost unreadable. In front of me was an L, an L which I'd put there. But the way the bottom bar curved up, you could have thought it was a U, and the bar was so small I suppose you might have assumed it was an I. Well, it was an L.

I thought about the pages of my handwriting I'd seen while I was packing my notebooks.

L. What was I thinking?

I thought about my patients. Every page I looked at, where there were only initials, no names, somebody else came to me. Someone talking to me; me talking to them. But you know what surprised me? It wasn't their voices, their sounds, as much as their silences and the way these had somehow remained with me. Those moments when we said nothing. Gaps. I thought about the things people do when they think they're being quiet: their movements, the way they shift in their seats. The rhythm of their breathing. Where they look. Where their thoughts go.

There was a young woman who said very little the whole time she was with me. I could see her as clearly as if she'd just walked out the door. Sometimes I mentioned to her the things I saw her do when she wasn't speaking. Mainly, it looked as if she was reading. She'd look at her palm, then turn to the back of her hand as if she was reading a paperback. She'd read up her wrists. When I asked her what was going on she looked at me as if I was mad.

Nothing, she said.

The way you look at your hand and wrist, I said.

It's nothing.

Eventually we talked about other things.

At the end of her treatment, as she was leaving the last session, we shook hands and I noticed a faint line of letters circling her wrist: words down the front and back of her fingers. What were they written in? Makeup? Eye liner? It was almost invisible. I saw a word: *empty*, and another: *crawl*.

What's that, I asked her, pointing with my finger. She laughed. *What do you mean?* I didn't say anything. Whatever

I had seen, the problem she had come to me with was no longer a worry. She felt free, she said. So she's free, I thought, with writing on her hands. That didn't seem so bad.

L.

My secretary put her head around the door; I jumped at the flash of blond hair. Suddenly, there was the smell of her perfume and the sense of someone else in the room before she could say a word. 'They're closing the tube.'

Silence. 'Sorry?'

'The roads are blocked.' Her face remained, intruding.

'Snow,' I said. I had been staring out at the snow, but it still seemed so unlikely.

'Look.' She smiled, the kind of smile you reserve for somebody you don't understand at all.

Beneath me a taxi chugged towards the lights at Cavendish Square, crawling and sliding.

'I've cancelled your appointments.'

I told her she'd better go home.

'What about you?'

'I'm all right' – and she went. Nicola, that was her name. I listened: her bag zipping, a quick tap of her keyboard, message sent, the little nibbling noise of her fingers on her mobile phone and the door closing; the latch clicking. I relaxed. Nicola. Gone.

Crack. I heard something, there in the room with me.

It was paper uncrumpling.

I was on my own.

I turned around, took in the boxes, and found myself staring at the books on the wall opposite me. I hadn't even started with them. Collections of letters: I have many volumes of letters. The usual rack of psychoanalytic literature – and poems. I collect first editions. That one, for example. My gaze fell on a book with a brown leather binding and faded gold type, not so different from many of the others, but in some way it stood out: *Pacchiarotto, and How He Worked in Distemper.* Why had it caught my eye, that peculiar title? What had led me there? Had somebody given it to me? I couldn't remember. Browning: I love Browning, but had *I* bought *that*?

I took it from the shelf and opened it at random. *St Martin's Summer.* I read out loud from the middle of the poem:

> *Ask else Penelope, Ulysses –*
> *Old in youth!*

Penelope. I thought of Browning's son: Pen, the wastrel. Of Penelope waiting faithfully for Ulysses to return. I read the whole poem quietly to myself and thought about Browning: his affair with Lady Ashburton after his wife, Elizabeth, died. In the poem he's writing about the impossibility of finding new love while he was still haunted by a past love.

Ghost-bereft, he writes at the end. *Ghost-bereft*: what's that? *Ghost-bereft*: a past love, still here. Love which can't be left behind.

Did he propose marriage to Lady Ashburton and break it off? Or was she keener chasing him than Browning was to follow? Maybe it wouldn't have mattered so much to him if his own father hadn't been chased through the courts for breach of promise. It had been all over the newspapers. Why was all this history, this ragged, unhappy biography, coming to me now?

Browning didn't want to end up like his father. I closed the book and placed it more heavily than I meant in the wooden box closest to the door. The box for my cellar: cool, dry and completely out of the way.

It wasn't the day to begin thinking about all of that. I had to think about moving. One book out of the way in – what? An hour's packing. That wasn't going to get me anywhere.

I went back to the window and thought about where I was heading. It was only up the street. I'd had my eye on the place ever since I'd moved where I was; for twenty-five years. Most mornings as I made my way through Regent's Park I entertained at least some fantasy about the buildings along the outer circle. The ones which looked in on the park.

For a moment, I imagined myself standing at one of those windows looking out onto ... well, if I'm honest, it might be the women. My mind still takes me in that direction even if, these days, I've worked out the rest of me doesn't have to follow. I daydreamed walking through the park at lunch time, being amongst all of those women, maybe catching the occasional eye and exchanging a certain smile – perhaps heading down to the canal or the zoo. All harmless. I felt sad. Sometimes, even now, I wonder about lost opportunities, about mistakes and the things I could have said.

Of course underneath all of this procrastination there was a very simple fact. However hard I thought about it there wasn't any real reason why I was moving. Whatever I conjured up to justify my move in the end, I had to admit, it was a matter of *why not*?

I laughed out loud and looked at a black and white photograph above the fireplace behind my desk: a big old Victorian house beside a church, half hidden by ancient oak trees. I'd taken that in late summer, when the leaves on the oaks were starting to turn. Through the leaves and the spindly branches there was a glimpse of the gravel path. I remembered the black door and the brass key on the inside and how strange it had felt the first time I went there, locking the door behind me.

This was Blanca's house. My Blanca, my old supervisor. How lonely I felt going there. Lonely, I thought, in the same way I felt that afternoon. Lonely and sad. When I opened the door to Blanca's room, though, that loneliness fell away; as it did when I thought about her. I laughed again, remembering how different our first meeting had been.

She sat opposite me, old in a way that was impossible to read. The thought had come to me, once, that the doctor or nurse who'd first taken hold of her when she was born – a cryptic East European baby – might have wondered: *aren't you a little old to be here*?

We sat in silence until I realised it was up to me to start speaking. Just like therapy, then. I was so new to it all.

'So,' I said, 'thank you for agreeing to supervise me. I'm really glad.'

'Really?' She scribbled something on the notepad balanced on her lap. It looked precarious, as if it was resting almost entirely on her left leg and if she moved ... how could she write like that? 'You are staring at my leg,' she said.

'No, sorry, I was–'

She cut across me.

'And I have not agreed to supervise you.'

I felt sick. 'But ...'

She stared at me. 'I agreed on the telephone, if you remember, to a meeting where we would discuss the possibility of us working together.' She wrote something else. 'Given your apparently naive, possibly rather infantile, desire to do so. Please, think back to our conversation.' She stopped speaking.

After a few seconds I tried to start again. 'Sorry.'

'Why are you apologising? You've been here five minutes and you've apologised to me twice. Do you really believe you've done something you need to apologise for?'

'No, I–'

'Well, then.' More silence.

So I tried a third time. 'Maybe you could tell me something about what you expect from me?'

'Mr Katiwa,' – it was to be at least a year before she began calling me Christopher – another six months before that became Chris – 'I only ask that you are as present as a person can be, that you listen to whoever you are talking to, in this case me, that you begin to listen in every way you can imagine, and that you are specific, and correct, when you report those conversations to me or anybody else.' She paused. 'Although whoever else that may be I do not know, as your work is completely confidential.' She sighed, tapping her pen. 'Bringing all of this to bear on what we are doing here, right now, I am still waiting for you to think about our telephone conversation where I agreed we would meet and discuss our working together. Do you understand?'

I made what I thought was a bold move. 'You sound angry.'

'No shit, Sherlock.' She shook her head. 'I do hope that in your practice you aspire to better things.'

I wished, I truly wished, that the chair I was sitting on would carry me away. Worse followed. As she glared at me I noticed her writing pad start to slide from her leg. I didn't say anything. It fell to the floor with a soft thud, its pages splayed. She looked down at it as I imagined she might at a pet dog who'd disgraced himself on the pavement. Then she looked at me.

'Why didn't you say anything?'

More shame. My cheeks almost steamed with heat. 'I didn't know what to ... do.'

'Do?' She sounded furious. 'As a psychoanalytic psychotherapist you do nothing at all. This isn't about helping anybody, Mr Katiwa. Let's be extremely clear about that from the very start. This is about *you*,' she jabbed her pen towards me, 'noticing *that*.' She flicked it down like a wand. I half-expected the notepad to become a frog. 'In fact I was interested that you did nothing.' She smiled, her mood seeming to have changed completely. 'Just as you said nothing.'

I replied very quietly, feeling broken. 'I was frightened.'

'Good,' she said. 'Very good, Mr Katiwa. Now we are getting *real* about things I think we can work together. Would you like to work with me?'

She had been recommended to me as one of the best supervisors in London. I took a breath, pressed my feet down onto the floor and replied as honestly as I could. 'No.'

She beamed: the Cheshire cat. Her smile couldn't have been any broader. Her face seemed to glow. Suddenly she was beautiful. 'Excellent. I suggest that we meet here every week at this time. Does that suit you?'

I nodded. The time did suit me.

And that was Blanca whom I think, somehow, I really came to love. When she died I couldn't work for a month. I cried almost every day. Blanca.

I took the picture down from the wall and put it in a cardboard box next to my desk: a box for my new consulting room. Blanca's house would go over the fireplace there, too.

For no reason I could think of my attention fell on the little red model of the Blackpool Tower on my desk. There we were in the room together, me and it. I stared at its china-blue top, dreamy somehow, but also rather squat. Dreamy enough to keep my mind stuck for a moment, holding me there, nowhere really, thinking: look at it, a scoop of ice-cream on the end of a cornet; and I thought of a real tower – a stone tower in Pisa, a clock tower rising above a swimming pool, the sun glittering on the water, nobody swimming there; and the old hotel beside it; and a valley of olive trees, morello cherries, and the swell of birdsong at dawn.

L.

I'd written an L on the window, and –

I looked out of the window.

No, there was L.

I stared back at the tower. It had belonged to my father and had been in a box – where? A box in the attic. In the loft. I felt my pulse beat under my watch strap.

When I cleared my father's house after he died, there had been several boxes in the attic containing things he used to have around him at work. Most were full of papers. I found them by accident under a tarpaulin next to the water tank, right above the eaves. Everything else had been taken out: a few bags of my mother's books, discoloured and dotted with mould; some empty suitcases I recognised from family holidays. The suitcases were strange to shift, like drums – hollow, fastened shut with old metal catches of a kind you don't see any more. I couldn't bear to open them. It was enough to hear they were empty.

Even with all of that gone the attic had still felt as if there was something in it. As if the air was still being used. I wondered if one of the cats had found its way up the ladder. There were three left when Dad died: angry little things that darted around the house, eluding me. Like flies, and just as hard to catch.

I shone my torch about, found the corner of the tarpaulin, lifted it, and discovered the boxes. Tea crates, lined with white paper. I pulled them out, one at a time, and rummaged through affidavits, letters, notes, and transcripts. Records of the court cases Dad spent most of his life wrapped up in.

He wasn't a barrister. He was a printer and that model of Blackpool tower had sat on the desk in his office at his workshop in London Bridge. It and a couple of other ornaments had lain crushed at the bottom of one of the boxes, tied up in a drawstring bag. The other two were beyond saving. For some reason, though, the tower was still in one piece. I adopted it. I took it into work and placed it on my desk in Harley Street. That little tower. The only thing of his I kept.

Dad. How had I ended up thinking about him? For a moment I was back in his office at London Bridge, staring at the angel fish gliding in the long, shallow aquarium at one end of his office. Sometimes when I sat there I wrote things. A poem came to me: *The Prayer of the Cat Who Bows in the Doorway*. When I wrote it I'd written Kat, not cat, because of my name:

I say fuck you to sun
I say fuck you to moon
I say fuck you to stars
I say fuck you to you
Fuck you.

My father. I never thought much about him, or my mother. They were dead and I was much happier for it. What was my father doing, getting into my work again?

The evening was drawing in. I turned on the light and went back to the boxes I had been looking through, throwing away loose sheets of paper, the occasional indecipherable scribble – keeping my attention focused on what I was doing. My scrawl.

*

At six I realised how late it was, that it had grown dark outside, and threw on my coat and hat in a rush. I tied my scarf, clattered down the stairs, opened the door to go home – and saw the snow: knee-deep and still quietly piling up. There was no wind. No noise. Cars stood abandoned, run into each other, skidded over the kerb and silently being smothered the whole length of Harley Street. I listened, my breath steaming in front of me.

I moved onto the step, not quite into the snow but onto a tiny strip of marble that remained uncovered, and glanced towards Cavendish Square as the traffic lights turned green. Something was moving down there – a person? The lights turned amber, and then red. I kept looking. What was that? More movement, slowly this time, inching out of the shadows around the railings. A fox. The animal looked briefly at me, stood very still, before heading into Wigmore Street. By the time the lights reached green again my face was numb. I was jumpy – stupidly so. Something about all that packing had unsettled me.

I went back inside, closed the door and stood by the reception desk, peering into the stairwell. I felt alone, disconnected. I switched on the lamp on the receptionist's desk. A newspaper lay next to a tiny Christmas tree and I read the headline, warning of the snow. I felt less lonely, but haunted, as if I'd done something wrong, and I stood there for a moment, thinking about that feeling. Had I done anything wrong? My attention returned to the model and then, I couldn't stop myself, to Pisa.

Another thought came to me, something I had never seen, but which had still left its mark. Something someone had described to me. A painting lying on the floor in an empty room; a picture of a villa in the Tuscan countryside, some of it scored away, the paint scraped off, right down to the canvas. I pressed my palms over my eyes. I didn't want those memories creeping in. Seeping in like gas, insidious and all around me.

I caught sight of the orange light from the street reaching under the door and hurried back upstairs.

CHAPTER 2
HARLEY STREET, 2010

Nicola's office felt like a haven. I sat on her chair and drank a coffee, glad that the door to my room was closed – that the tower was out of sight. I smelled the air: she must have put on some perfume before she'd left. I recognised it: Rive Gauche. You don't sit in rooms with hundreds of men and women over the years and not get to know their perfumes.

She'd asked me once, was I married, and I told her I wasn't. Perhaps she expected a story or maybe she expected more than that.

I drank my coffee, contemplating the night ahead, still wearing my overcoat because the heating appeared to have turned itself off. I glanced around at the Christmas cards on the window ledges, at the silver and gold tinsel framing the photographs on the wall beside the door. I switched on the electric heater and listened to it whir.

Behind Nicola's desk there was an old wooden cupboard.

I opened it.

The top shelf was full of stationery: large manila envelopes, packets of record cards and letter-headed paper. The next had a scattering of personal things, all of them Nicola's. A bottle of Rive Gauche, like I thought. Nothing much on the third one down, or the one below. Odds and ends. But the bottom shelf ...

I hesitated. I knew very well what was on the bottom shelf, at the back, behind some junk, because I had put it there years before, burying it. I bent down and reached for it. An old envelope. I touched it. It wasn't sealed. I pulled it out, rehearsing in my mind the three words I knew would be written on it – not in my handwriting, but in Simon's: *The Eleventh Letter*. I sat cross-legged on the floor and emptied the contents in front of me. Two old C-120 cassette tapes fell onto the carpet, one with a typed label: *'Louise: Pisa'*, and the other with the label handwritten: *'Louise: Pisa, second time'*. The writing was faded on both.

I got up and walked to the window. No writing on that one. The glass felt cold even before I put my cheek on it, trying to soothe myself, and I stared into the sky above the street lights: closed, dark, inaccessible; still snowing. I looked down onto the street – perhaps a movement caught my eye, like the one I had seen earlier, in the shadows towards Cavendish Square – and I noticed a woman in a fur coat standing there, waiting on the steps of the building opposite, staring at me.

I wanted to hide, but she'd seen me. I looked at her. She must have been freezing: the coat was short and her legs bare, as if she was wearing a party dress underneath. Her calves disappeared into the snow like a bird's legs, a wader just offshore. I knocked on the glass.

She stared at me, confused – dazed, as though she'd just woken up. She smiled nervously and nodded in a way that somehow felt expected. There was something about her smile, something inevitable, in the way you might see someone walking towards you, in the distance, down a long straight path, and know well before your paths crossed that you would eventually have to acknowledge each other with a nod, a smile, or a polite word. But I'd never seen her before. I was sure of it.

I tapped again and waved, pointing towards the front door beneath me. Her head shifted, something like a nod, and she began to cross the road, picking her way awkwardly through the snow. I hurried from the room, made my way down the stairs again, and threw the door open. She was standing on the step, blinking.

I didn't know what to say. What I was about to say, I wanted to swallow back. *Not just now*, I wanted to say – *not now*. 'Come in,' she heard me say. And she glanced into the hall – not quite aware of me, I thought. Perhaps she wasn't well. What kind of a person would go out in the snow dressed like that? Her face looked bluish, which I took to be from the cold, although there weren't any other signs: no trembling; no shivering even though her long red hair was full of snow. She seemed rather relaxed. Dazed, I told myself.

'Please,' I said. 'Come in.'

Bowing her head, she pushed past me. She had to. I might have invited her inside but I was blocking her path as surely as the snow outside had blocked mine. She looked around and raised her head a little, as if she was aware of something.

'You're very kind,' she said, her voice soft, like a bird's feather. Down.

'Not at all.'

She brushed her hand through her hair, so clumps of snow fell on the floor, onto the rug, melting.

'Don't worry,' I told her.

'Sorry?'

'The rug,' I said.

'Oh, the rug.'

She was slim and very slight. The bird I'd imagined, the wader as I saw her standing in the snow, was close to the mark. She slipped her coat off. Underneath she wore a short, expensive-looking black dress. It was as if she had been to a party.

'You must have been cold out there.'

She removed her gloves slowly, as if she was thinking about something, and put them in her coat pocket. There was a grey silk scarf around her neck that she didn't touch.

Eventually she acknowledged my presence again, as though she'd been lost in her thoughts. 'Sorry?'

'Not much of an evening for a walk,' I said.

'No. Actually I wasn't walking anywhere.'

'You weren't?'

'I kind of found myself here – there.' She waved her hand back towards the road and peered at me, as if she was doing her best to remember something. 'Do I know you?' she asked.

I told her she didn't.

'It's kind of you to invite me in.' She took a breath and rubbed her eyes. 'But kind of odd? Sorry, it's very kind of you to invite me in.'

'I expect it's the cold.'

'The cold?' It was as if she hadn't noticed the snow. Maybe she was in shock.

'Well, wherever I am, I'm here. Where am I?'

'Harley Street.'

'Harley Street. In London?'

She might as well have stepped out of a time machine. I needed to get her inside, take her up to my room and see how I could help.

'My consulting rooms on the third floor are reasonably comfortable. They're warm, at least – better than being out there.'

Something suddenly seemed to shift, as if she were more awake. 'Yes. I see what you mean: of course, the snow.' It had dawned on her why I was talking about the cold. 'It's awful,' she said. 'You wouldn't get a car down the street. The third floor?' She studied my name and qualifications on the brass plate behind the reception desk. 'Christopher Katiwa. You're a psychiatrist?'

I nodded, starting towards the stairs. 'Yes, qualified as. But I practise as a psychotherapist, mostly.'

'Shall we go up?' She was already moving towards the stairs.

I nodded uncertainly, following her as she began to climb them.

'I'm on the third floor,' I said.

'Yes. You said.'

She hurried up them. I started to grow breathless and found myself several steps behind her by the time we reached the top.

'Here?' She pointed to the door with my name on it.

'Yes –' I managed to step in front of her and caught hold of the door handle. That was better. This was *my* place. I steadied myself and caught my breath.

When I turned the handle I was struck by how warm it already was inside. I was pleased to see the door to my office closed, as if it was like that through foresight, and I led her into Nicola's room instead.

She went to the window and looked straight down onto the street. 'Is this the window you saw me from?' Her hands were clasped, as if she was expecting something to happen.

'Yes, it is.' I waited a moment, wondering if she would say any more. She didn't. I told her to take a seat and went to make some tea. When I got back she had settled on one of the two comfortable chairs facing each other. The ones which I occasionally sat in when I assessed a patient in there. I took my coat off, closed the door, sat in the other and reintroduced myself.

'My name's Kay,' she said. 'It's very nice up here.' She sipped her tea.

I told her something about what usually went on in the rooms around us and asked what she did.

She hesitated. 'I travel.' A lie, I thought.

She grinned as though she'd read my mind and corrected herself. 'That's almost what I do.'

'You almost travel?'

'I'd rather not say exactly what I do.' She spoke easily, unembarrassed. 'To say I travel is true ...' She looked at me, summing something up. 'It's true enough.' She looked down into her tea, then back at me. 'You're a psychiatrist and a psychotherapist?'

'That's right.'

She kicked off her shoes and adjusted the scarf around her neck. 'They're wet,' she sighed. 'What a peculiar situation.'

'Are you okay?' I asked.

'It was a shock finding myself out there.'

'I'm sure.'

She noticed the tapes I had emptied onto the floor and looked at me.

'I'm packing up.'

'Packing?' She noticed some crates standing against the wall. 'Moving?'

'Yes.'

'Why on earth would you want to move from here?'

I couldn't think what to say. 'There isn't any single reason.'

'No?'

Something about her insistence worried me. I blushed. Her silence: her gaze between me and the tapes.

'I'm restless,' I said. 'I'm getting older.'

'Where are you moving to?'

'Somewhere bigger.'

'Isn't this large enough?'

'It doesn't feel that way.'

'Oh.' I couldn't work out what she meant by that.

'I'm rather tired,' I said. 'Something about all this packing.' I didn't want her there.

'And I'm an unwanted visitor.'

Again, it was as if she had read my mind. 'Unexpected, but not unwanted.'

'Unwanted, I think.'

I was about to correct her again but stopped myself, got up and went to the window instead. 'All of this snow,' I said. It was falling as heavily as ever, covering any signs of life as quickly as they appeared. There was no trace of Kay, of where she had been standing, or her steps across the street to my front door.

She was at the window beside me.

'What were you doing out there?' I asked.

She shrugged. I studied her as she gazed onto the street, as she blinked. There was something on her mind. When, eventually, she spoke her voice was softer: 'It's unexpected, don't you think, being stranded like this in the middle of London?'

'Unexpected? Yes, I suppose it is.'

'We won't be going anywhere for a while.'

We faced each other. Maybe she was older than I'd thought; close up, like that, I realised she might almost have been the same age as me – young-looking but still there were faint lines, creases like you'd find on the pages of a book, smoothed out even if they had once been folded; lines reaching from the corners of her eyes, around her mouth, and across her forehead.

At the same moment, in perfect synchronicity, we returned to our chairs.

She pointed to the cassette tapes. 'Can I ask what they are?'

I didn't say anything.

'Something you found while you were packing?'

Why had I left them on the floor like that? 'Sorry.' I leaned forward to pick them up. 'I should have put them away.'

'You assumed you'd be on your own.'

I did, but what was I doing, getting them out in the first place?

'Can we listen to them?' she asked.

I was shocked. 'We can't do that.'

'They look very old.'

I stared at them, transparent plastic, the little sliver of tape visible along the base. 'It's my work.' I touched one of the cassettes, just for a moment, the one with the handwriting on it. My handwriting.

'You want to respect somebody's privacy.'

I thought about the last time I'd listened to the tapes, years before, and something inside me contracted, like a hand closing. What were we doing? I felt guilty and ashamed. My chest burned.

'Even now?' she asked.

Even now? It really was as if she could hear me thinking.

'It's so long ago. Do you have a tape player?' she asked.

'What?'

'Shall I look in the cupboard?'

'Shall you what? No –' I was insistent, 'it really wouldn't be right.' It felt like an attack.

'Let's look for something to play them on.' She went to the cupboard, ignoring me.

'You can't go in there.'

'Your hand,' she said, pointing at me.

My hand was open, shaking, above the tapes. I drew it back, pushing it into my pocket. 'What are you doing?' I felt crushed.

'We can listen to the tapes.'

'No.' Things were moving too fast. I absolutely, madly wanted to listen to them. Of course I did. But I knew that, on my own, the chances were I almost certainly wouldn't. Perhaps I would even destroy them. So what she was doing, of course it was what I wanted. But we couldn't.

'You want to listen to them on your own.'

We couldn't.

She found the tape recorder without really having to look for it, as if she knew exactly where it was, brought it back, and plugged it in. It was a plain little black machine about the size of a hardback novel. The kind you found in most offices twenty-five years ago: portable, durable, effective, with a built-in microphone. It was the same one I'd taken with me when –

'Shall I?' she asked. 'You need some help with this.'

'What?' My thoughts telescoped. I was far away, watching Louise swim in the pool on the terrace, in the sun. I started to climb the stone steps.

In Harley Street, Kay and I were a little dot of consciousness, a speck I was barely aware of. She was kneeling on the floor, an insect, holding the cassette with the type-written label.

'I'm assuming this is the right order?' she asked again. 'This one first? The one with the typed label?' What a tiny voice.

I think I said yes. I heard the compartment on top open and close. A hiss filled the air like the noise of heavy rain, then two sharp clicks, and a sound like material tearing. Kay stood listening, her eyes fixed on something far away. She said: 'Somebody's touching the microphone.'

She returned to her seat.

I tried to get up, to end the whole thing, but Louise started speaking.

CHAPTER 3
PISA, 1986

LOUISE [Vacantly.]
Huh?

SIMON [His voice is rich, deep, young again.]
Where were you then, Louise? What were you thinking of?

LOUISE [Gently, her voice subtle and soft, as if she has all the time she wants.]
When Kate and I were students.

SIMON
When you were both at Oxford?

LOUISE
Kate was late getting home one evening. It was a Sunday. The middle of winter. I was sitting in the living room waiting

for her, watching the clock – feeling worried. She said she'd be back by five and that we'd cook dinner together. The fire was burning down. I remember ... glancing over and thinking: shall I put another log on? But I sat where I was. I had a book.

I can't remember which one and I don't remember reading it, only holding it and wondering where she was. I looked at the fire again and it was glowing, still smoking, and I remember thinking that was the last chance I'd have to stoke it up. I sat there and it died.

SIMON
What time was this?

LOUISE
Eight.

SIMON
That isn't late. Why were you worrying?

LOUISE
I don't know. I had a feeling, a terrible feeling. I've never been sure what it was about.

SIMON
She'd been late before?

LOUISE
Yes.

SIMON
So why worry?

LOUISE

I don't know. At about half past eight I heard a key in the front door. She threw it open and hurried in calling my name. I didn't answer, I was so angry. I sat there, smouldering. She went up to my room, then down into the kitchen, calling out. At last she came into the living room. 'There you are.' She was breathless, smiling.

'What do you mean?' I remember how cold my voice sounded. It shocked me. I hadn't said a word since I'd sat down. My throat was tight. She was smiling and I shouted at her.

I said, 'Where the fuck have you been?' She asked what I meant and pointed at the clock. She said it was half past eight. I screamed something; she shouted back and stormed up to bed. I sat there another hour, waiting for her to come down. She didn't. I went up to my room, half-expecting her to come knocking on the door, which I slammed so she knew for sure I was there.

She didn't knock. I heard her crying; and I was thinking I'd go in to see her – only I must have been tireder than I thought because the next thing I knew I was waking the next morning, still in my clothes, stretched out on my bed.

SIMON

What was going on?

LOUISE *[Shaky, hesitant]*

I was being needy. I wasn't myself.

SIMON

Why are you telling me this?

LOUISE

I felt terrible waking up like that and I went straight through to see Kate. She was sitting on her bed reading – the door was half open. I asked if I could come in. She looked at me but didn't say anything. I saw she'd been crying. I told her how sorry I was. She still didn't say anything. She didn't say a word until I started crying, then she scrambled off the bed and hugged me, crying too. We stood there for ages saying how sorry we were to each other.

Eventually we were hugging each other, really tight, wrapped round each other, our faces stuck together with tears.

I could see the bed over her shoulder and her book lying open on it. I asked what she was reading and she told me it was Jack France. She'd been to a bookshop and found the book there. She'd started reading it when she got to the bus stop, sitting on a bench under a street light, and got lost in it. So lost she didn't notice the rain, or the buses coming and going. All the time I'd been sitting waiting for her in the front room she'd been sitting reading Jack France's poetry at the bus stop, getting wet. She told me she'd never read anything like it.

I tried reading him but he didn't have the same effect on me.

[Silence, for several seconds.]

Well, that was that. He became something of an obsession for her.

SIMON
I see.

LOUISE [Irritated, perhaps.]
Yes.

SIMON
What about the telephone call?

LOUISE [Hesitant, distracted.]
What do you mean?

SIMON
Before you started talking about Kate getting back late you said were going to tell me about the telephone call she received when she was in the garden at Wasing.

LOUISE
About her and John's honeymoon. Yes, I know.

SIMON
Can you tell me about how Kate and John ended up in Italy?

[Silence]

You said Kate was in the garden at Wasing and the phone rang. Maybe you could begin there?

LOUISE
There's a lot more to it than that.

SIMON
Tell me everything then.

LOUISE
This is last summer. Ten years after we were at Oxford.

SIMON
Last summer.

LOUISE
Kate told me she was in the garden when she got the call about her honeymoon. She was staring into the lily pond, I think. She said she'd seen something strange.

[A lengthy silence, then she speaks more quickly, as if she's been gathering her thoughts.]

SIMON
What was that?

LOUISE *[Distracted.]*
Sorry?

SIMON *[Impatiently.]*
What did she see?

LOUISE
When I think about it, it's strange.

[Silence.]

I can remember so much of it. It feels so full of detail, as though I can see it all close up.

SIMON
Then tell me the detail.

LOUISE
The grass around her was very long. And she was crouching down, her dress spread out around her like ... so that ... if

you'd been watching her from up above she'd have looked like a flower.

SIMON
From above?

LOUISE
Yes.

SIMON
From the sky?

LOUISE
Yes.

SIMON
Why would anyone be watching her from the sky?

LOUISE [Silence.]
I asked her that as well. It was so weird.

SIMON
What did she say?

LOUISE
She laughed, as though she didn't expect me to believe her. But she knew I was the one person she could *always* rely on to believe her.

SIMON
I see.

LOUISE
She told me about a dream she'd had, the week before, the night after she'd arrived at Wasing to get things sorted out for the wedding. In the dream, there was a flower.

SIMON
What kind of a flower?

LOUISE
In her dream she could only see the flower from the sky. Down on the ground, there was just its shadow.

SIMON
There was nothing there.

LOUISE *[As if she her thoughts had drifted.]*
What?

[Silence.]

SIMON
I was repeating what you said.

LOUISE
You said there was nothing there. That's not right. There was a shadow.

[Silence.]

I want to describe her dream. It explains –
[Silence.]

SIMON
What does it explain?

LOUISE
I don't know.

[Silence.]

From the ground the flower looked like a shadow. Of course it didn't make sense. It was a dream. When she woke up the next morning and looked out of the bedroom window she was sure she could see it, the shadow, or something exactly like it, for real, out of her dream, at the end of the garden. But then, when she saw it, it looked as though it was a person's shadow. Not a flower. It was as if there was somebody standing there.

[Silence.]

SIMON
Somebody?

LOUISE
Yes, that's right. As if someone was there. But there was just a shadow.

[The sound of her voice changes, as if there is suddenly more distance between her and the microphone; as though she has drawn back.]

The moment she noticed the shadow, it vanished.

SIMON
It vanished.

LOUISE
Yes. As if the sun had become brighter and ... it dissolved.
Every morning after that she felt sure she saw it again, out
of the corner of her eye. The moment she tried to pick it out
properly, though, it went.

SIMON
You think that's important?

LOUISE
Something was bothering her.

SIMON
She wasn't herself.

LOUISE
Yes. She thought there was someone watching her.

SIMON
Are you suggesting that what's happened ... Kate and John's
disappearance ... may have something to do with what she
told you about this shadow? Are you questioning her state
of mind?

LOUISE *[Confused. The sound of her breath is audible.]*
No. I'm trying to describe it. I mean ...

[Silence.]

SIMON
What do –

LOUISE *[Cutting across him, her voice much louder than it has been. She speaks more quickly.]*
Kate said her mornings started to revolve around a particular routine. She'd get up, wash herself, dress and look out of the window for the shadow. She'd catch sight of it and then lose it so quickly she could never be quite certain if it had been there at all.

[Silence, then when she speaks her voice is softer once more.]

The morning she heard about the honeymoon was different.

[Silence. A long wait before Simon speaks.]

SIMON
How do you mean?

LOUISE
It changed.

[Silence.]

SIMON *[More gently.]*
What happened?

LOUISE
That morning, after she dressed ...

[Seems to hesitate. Voice dies away. Then more freely, but still with a kind of constraint. As though she is being guarded. Her words are a beat behind what she is thinking.]

... she looked out of the window and couldn't see what she was looking for – there wasn't a shadow. There were the trees and the flowers, and the long grass.

[That dreamy, detached quality to her voice returns: gliding.]

It was a dull day but there were still weak shadows. The one she expected to see, though – it wasn't there. Then she noticed something about the pond.

There was something dark in the water: *a shadow*. As soon as she saw it, it seemed to come apart, losing its edges like a cloud of ink, swirling and shifting.

She ran downstairs to the conservatory and stared out through the French windows. It was still there. She was scared: she wanted to get away. It felt as if something uncontrollable was about to happen, but she couldn't move –

[Louise is breathing hard. The sound is very clear. She mutters something indistinct.]

SIMON
What is it?

LOUISE *[Breathless, a whisper.]*
She was so scared.

[Sound of a sob.]

If she moved she was sure something dreadful would happen.

SIMON
It's OK.

LOUISE *[Ignoring him.]*
She saw the telephone behind her handbag on the breakfast table and slowly reached for it. She took a step and, like a blink, like an eye opening, the thing in the water grew – really fast, filling the whole pond, lapping against the edges. She couldn't look away; she found the phone – but the thing in the water, whatever it was disappeared.

The surface of the water glittered. The sun had come through the clouds.

[Silence.]

There were shadows from the branches on the trees, the flowers, the grass. And there was the house: Wasing. Grand, white, bold in the light. She thought: there, that's where the shadow came from. Wasing.

She unlocked the French windows, pushed them apart and stepped into the humid morning air. She walked down to the pond and crouched down, feeling her dress spread around her. She said she felt like she was the flower in her dream and that, at that moment, she could see herself from above – just like she had in her dream. She felt sick, as if she'd been drinking champagne.

[Silence, several seconds.]

I think I began here.

SIMON
Yes. You were going to tell me about Kate's honeymoon getting cancelled.

LOUISE
I've gone round in a circle.

[Almost silence: both of them are moving, small movements, shifting a foot, folding their arms, perhaps.]

I'd rather not say any more.

[Silence.]

SIMON
You said she went into the garden.

LOUISE
Yes.

SIMON
The phone call about the honeymoon.

LOUISE [Distracted.]
I know.

SIMON
Why is the honeymoon being cancelled important?

LOUISE [Snaps at him.]
Because that's why they ended up in Italy. I want to stop now.

SIMON
You said she went into the garden.

LOUISE
No, I want to stop here.

[Sound of movement, footsteps, a click, a moment of complete silence on the tape followed by another click. Simon speaks. It sounds as if he is very near the microphone. Background noise and subsequent comments suggest he is having breakfast at his hotel.]

SIMON
Summary of yesterday's session, which finished early. Louise ended the session abruptly. I believe she's lying. A defence against ... who knows what. I can't imagine getting any closer to the truth than the police have. Semproni, the man in charge of the case, claims that she's fucked in the head. He says he doesn't know if she's guilty. Maybe she's both. The detail in what she says, the descriptions of what Kate is thinking and feeling seem implausible as memories of whatever Kate may have said to her. If Kate said anything to her at all. In fact I approach the next session with very little idea of what Kate may have been thinking or feeling, or John. The detail, I imagine, is what she creates as she fabricates, as she fantasises. I don't believe it was what she was told. Wasing. The dream she describes Kate having. I imagine her envy. Her envy of Kate and I imagine we'll see this play out. Her envy for Kate as a more successful academic; her envy for Kate having John. Her envy of them as a couple and her desire to destroy what she can't have. All very sad. Anyway: kippers for breakfast. Joan –

[Our secretary at the time.]

Very good of you to book me in here. Good English breakfast thus far. Can you tell Chris to look out that piece by Bion on *lies* we discussed once? I have a distinct memory of it.

PISA. 1986

[Clink of china. Tea being poured.]

I imagine they may have been having an affair. Her and John. No, maybe her and Kate. I mean, she sounds as though she knew her way around. Probably knew Wasing inside out from going there to fuck him. Or her.

CHAPTER 4

HARLEY STREET, 2010

The cassette player stopped. The lights went off and the whirring of the electric heater died.

What had I done, letting her play the tapes? And what was this, now; a power cut? I muttered: 'Are you OK?'

Kay didn't reply.

I stared in the direction I knew she'd been sitting. It wasn't quite dark. A pale light shone through the window – the moon, reflecting off the snow – enough for me to see her face, but only to realise I could not see her face. It was as if I was staring at a mannequin – a face. An empty, expressionless face, one waiting for the gift of life.

I stood up.

'It's all right,' she said. 'I'm here.'

There was a flash, a flame – a cigarette lighter in front of her face. There she was, after all, facing me intently.

'Do you have any candles?' she asked.

I nodded, confused.

'Hurry up,' she said. 'My finger might burn.'

There were some candles in the cupboard. I fetched one and stood it on a book in the middle of the floor. She lit it.

'That's dangerous,' she said. I looked around; there was an old ashtray, a silver dish with an army insignia that Nicola used for paper clips. I tipped them out, put it under the candle.

I looked out of the window. The street lights were off.

Why was I letting her take control like this?

'Because it's what you want,' she said.

'How do you know that – what you just said?'

'Because it's obvious. What are we listening to?'

'I'd rather not say.'

'The man says the woman's lying. Louise?'

'Yes, Louise. It's an interview,' I said.

'He says she's lying,' she repeated.

'Yes, he does.'

'Was she?' She got up and started rummaging in the desk.

'What are you looking for?'

'Some batteries. You want to keep listening. Don't you?' She shut the top drawer hard. I closed my eyes.

'What's his name?' she said.

'Simon.'

She tried the next drawer: staples, some labels – an unopened packet of batteries. She tore the card off the back and two fell out into her hand. 'Why did you want to listen to it?'

'Why do you insist on wanting to know? I'm moving. I was packing and I remembered the tapes.'

She made a sound as if she was holding back saying something, then picked up the tape recorder and loaded the batteries. She made the sound again.

'What?'

'Why are you moving?' she asked, leaning towards me before I could press play. She crossed her legs and clasped her knee.

'I don't understand why you're asking me.'

'Earlier, when I asked you why you'd ever want to move from here you didn't seem very sure.'

Outside I could hear someone trying to start an engine. It turned over once and died.

'There isn't any particular reason.'

'No?' A pause.

'Do you think,' she began, 'that you might have decided to move so you could find the tapes?'

'What?' I felt cold; very cold.

'Burningly it came on me all at once, this was the place.'

'What?'

'Browning.'

'I know. Robert Browning. I've heard it before. Why are you quoting it to me?'

She reached across and pressed PLAY:

— around Wasing.

Simon's lost words sounded in front of us.

'You're saying I decided to move so I could find the tapes?'

'Perhaps.'

I closed my eyes. There was silence, the silence of the hiss of the tape.

Simon said something else, barely a syllable, and Louise began speaking. And he gave way, letting her speak. She continued to talk, her voice intense, tight, the pitch drifting.

I was moving so I could find the tapes?

It had been hard enough forgetting them.

CHAPTER 5
PISA, 1986

SIMON
Fuck it. Who knows? Let's wait and see.

[Click. Silence. Another click.]

LOUISE
I can't remember where we were.

SIMON *[Tired, bored.]*
You were describing Kate in the garden, the morning she heard her honeymoon was cancelled. She saw something *dark* in a pond.

LOUISE
Are you taking me seriously?

[Silence.]

Yes she was in the garden. And she was thinking about how far away she was from anyone, or anywhere. Wasing's lonely. There are fields round it – the empty kind. The woods are very old. There are no other houses. I couldn't have stayed there like she did, on her own. But she said she liked it.

SIMON
Did you believe her?

LOUISE
Perhaps, as far as she knew. I think she blocked things out. She sometimes retreated into her own little world.

[Silence.]

When the telephone rang she found herself staring towards the conservatory without knowing how long she'd been staring, and she jumped up and ran to it. And when she answered it, when she said hello, her voice sounded weak and distant, so different, she told me it was as if she couldn't even be sure it was her own. There was a hiss on the line. She took it outside.

[Silence.]

SIMON
I'm confused.

LOUISE
Kate took the phone outside, to the pond. She often did that; walked while she was talking, picking up the phone and letting the cord trail behind her. This is at Wasing, after she

saw the shape in the pond. Kate got a phone call about her honeymoon. I'm thinking about what they said. She spoke it out for me, his voice and hers, the whole conversation, like something on the radio.

SIMON
What did they say?

LOUISE
'Dr Baxter?' he asked.
  'Yes?'
  'Dr Baxter?' You could tell he was foreign straight away: Italian.
  'Yes?'
  'I am from *Hotel Roma*.'
  That was where they were booked to stay. 'Yes?' she said.
  He said he had some bad news.
  'Yes?' she asked.
  He said he was very sorry.
  'Sorry for what?'
  He told her there'd been a fire.
  She didn't know what to say. She looked up at the sky – caught the sun.
  He told her they'd had to close the hotel down.
  'No.'
  He said that he was sorry.
  'No.' She didn't believe him. 'No,' she said. 'We're staying at your hotel.'
  He told her that was impossible. She asked if they were double-booked.
  'No.' He told her about the fire again and the truth began to sink in.
  'What are we going to do?'

He didn't answer.

'What shall we do?'

He said one of his managers would call her. Kate said he sounded scared.

SIMON

She was very upset.

LOUISE

She told me she couldn't think straight; there were flashes in front of her eyes from the sun. She told him it was her honeymoon.

He told her he was sorry. Very sorry. And he was silent. She could hear him breathing.

She thumped the receiver down; the bell in the phone rang out once, plaintively and she stared into the pond at her own muddy reflection. What was she going to do? She had to tell John, but she couldn't think how.

And it felt as if someone was watching her.

She shouted out: 'Is anybody there?'

Something rustled in the lavender and a wren hopped out of a bush. A breeze blew gently on her face as she looked around the garden: the lavender bed; the tall daisies swaying as their stalks bent in the breeze. Anemones and lavender in one corner, and an old apple tree, its branches thick with new fruit. In another corner there were rhododendrons, glossy and wet-looking, slightly too close together.

[A pause: what she has said came as a steady stream of words. Now it seems as if she has run out of words.]

SIMON

You sound as though you really know the place.

LOUISE
Why do you say that?

SIMON
Don't you know it?

LOUISE
I only know it well because of Kate – and John. I've been there, but that's not the same. It's like me telling you all this. If you'd met Kate once or twice wouldn't you still know more about her after talking to me?

SIMON
Maybe I would.

LOUISE
You know there's so much she said about that place.

[Change of tone: surprise.]

I remember Kate telling me what a struggle it was to get there the first time she came to Wasing, with John. Just after she met him. They ended up having to walk through a field. Their car broke down.

SIMON
Can you remember any more?

LOUISE
Not really. They met his mother by accident, the first time, climbing over the fence to get into the house from the field.

[Silence.]

SIMON
What about the first time Kate met John? Can you remember that?

LOUISE
I remember it really well. It was at a Browning conference at the University of Kent. Unpleasant place. I was giving a paper: 'Dickens, Browning and the Mysterious Letter.' Dickens wrote a letter to one of his friends praising one of Browning's plays, but Browning never got to see it until after Dickens died. It caused some trouble between them. – Browning thought that Dickens hadn't supported him

SIMON
That was the first time you met John?

LOUISE
Yes, it was. Three years ago. Kate was there because she's a Browning person and John was there because of the Pen connection.

SIMON
I don't know about the *Pen* connection.

LOUISE
Pen was Robert Browning's son. Officially Pen didn't have any children, but unofficially he had an illegitimate son with a servant. That child was Jack France's great-grandfather. John was there to talk about the connection.

So Kate and I were in the audience and there was John, standing next to the film screen draped down over the blackboard in one of the lecture theatres, the lights dim and two faces on the screen: Browning and Jack France.

They didn't really look much alike. Browning had a beard; he looked kind of healthy, as if he took plenty of country walks – although I don't imagine he did that too often with Elizabeth around. Jack was pale and very thin. He hung out in the Hotel Ellington and the Paris Bar in Berlin, the kinds of place David Bowie and Iggy Pop hung out in a few years later. And John looked like neither, but was still rather lovely. As soon as she saw him I remember Kate's eyes opening – they did: they opened a little wider. He was wearing a black suit, his hair was short and he had a thin red tie. Like a cool-looking gallery owner – which is what he was. He had a good voice: soft but strong. Very deep. A kind of a rumble. You know? The way some voices get inside you. Kate liked that.

Five minutes after he started speaking he was looking at us, smiling. We were sitting a couple of rows back but I suppose we might have stood out. Most academics – they have a sort of aspic look. Or they're gross. We always said we got into it by mistake.

SIMON
How do you mean?

LOUISE
We looked good; we were friendly, but neither of us tried to make anything of it. And it felt as though he was giving the whole talk to us, which is what he eventually said he had done, anyway. It was good. The thing about his father and Robert Browning he'd said, if the stories about Pen are to be believed, if they were at all related; the thing that they shared in common, if you'd met them, he said, was that you'd not have known either was a poet. He stood between the two images, turning his face a little towards whoever

61

he was referring to. He quoted Thomas Hardy, who said Browning was like a grocer – someone so everyday you'd never guess he wrote as he did. He read from Henry James's story: 'A Private Life'. Then he quoted Bowie about Jack France, even though Bowie never actually met him. *Jack was like a cat you suddenly find in your kitchen, eating out of your cat's dish. But your cat doesn't seem to mind because there's something supercat about this cat, and you don't mind because for a while everyone wants a supercat around. Slinkier, funnier and more of a cat than any cat you've ever known. Until he eats you out of house and home, of course, and he pops next door, forgetting all about you, without even saying goodbye. That was Jack.*

SIMON
It sounds as if John didn't have a particularly high opinion of his father.

LOUISE
Henry James said there didn't have to be a link between a writer's personality and what he writes. That's how John summed up. You'd never know either of them from their writing. Maybe their letters are different.

After the talk, Kate and I started chatting to him. We went for a walk around the university grounds and stood looking down on the cathedral. I asked him: 'What was your father really like?' John looked confused. Kate blushed and said she was sorry. I wondered what was the matter. I tried to change the subject – said something silly, bland, about the campus being such a nice place. About the rabbits.

Kate nudged me. She knew something – she would do; she was obsessed with Jack France. John must have seen. He grinned and shook his head.

'It's all right,' he said to me. 'Perhaps I should have made it clearer in my talk. I never met my father. He died – he disappeared – a few months before I was born. He and my mother were honeymooning in Italy.' He said it exactly like that; so matter-of-fact.

I apologised. He put a hand on my shoulder and said it was all right. But he was looking at Kate while he did so, and she was looking at him as though they already knew each other.

'You're very kind,' Kate said.

I don't know what he replied. I can't remember. But he moved his hand from me and took hers.

SIMON
He took Kate's?

LOUISE
That's right.

SIMON
Was that difficult for you?

LOUISE
Difficult? [Long pause.] I liked him, obviously. But I don't expect every man I feel interested in to reciprocate.

[Silence.]

It isn't as though they abandoned me. We went for tea in Broadstairs, a little cake shop looking out onto the sea; it was foggy and the sea was like glass, and he told us about K.

SIMON
The book: *K*.

LOUISE
He was about to send the galleys off to his editor and he asked us if we cared to read them. Kate said she would.

SIMON
What about you?

LOUISE
I kept out of it, actually.

SIMON
You did?

LOUISE
It felt icky.

SIMON
Icky?

LOUISE
A son collects his father's letters to his lover and publishes them while his mother's still alive. That son never met his father.

SIMON
His mother was still alive?

LOUISE
She was, then, yes. And every letter, all ten of them, were written by Jack France while she was pregnant with John. But that's what John was like.

SIMON
What do you mean? *[Sounds impatient, a sigh after he finishes speaking.]*

LOUISE
I think he was angry.

SIMON
Why would he be angry?

LOUISE
You seem angry.

[Silence.]

All right. *[As if she is shrugging.]* Maybe you're not.

SIMON
Didn't you talk about it with Kate?

LOUISE
I told her I thought it was a dumb thing to do. She didn't agree with me. She thought the letters were important and she had a line on it: he's a collector. He doesn't make art; he makes money out of it.

SIMON
But this was about his father.

LOUISE
A lot of artists have made money out of their relationship with their parents. The more fucked up it was, the better. So maybe he was angry. If I was angry with my parents I'd

probably want to forget about them, I think. But that's just me. Whatever the reason, publishing the letters gave him some control. Kate agreed with that.

SIMON
Did she? What about what she did, then? What about what she did with the letters?

LOUISE
I don't want to talk about that.

SIMON
I'm thinking of the book Kate was writing: her replies to the letters in Jack France's *K*.

LOUISE
Let's move on.

SIMON
I think it's important.

LOUISE
She's an academic and there was a rationale.

SIMON
I find *that* icky. As if ...

LOUISE
What?

SIMON
As though she wanted to be K.

LOUISE *[Laughs dismissively.]*
I think that was rather the point. She was K. Kate. K can mean anybody because nobody knows who the real K was.

[Changes the subject.]

Do you want to know how John found the Villa Inghilterra?

SIMON *[Pauses.]*
If you like.

LOUISE
John found it by accident on his way to visit Christina.

SIMON *[Interested.]*
Who's Christina?

LOUISE
She was an old friend of his father's. An artist. A model. You know the kind of person; they usually end up doing something interesting. She owned a gallery in Camaiore, near Pisa, that John traded with. Every now and then he'd go there and stock up for his London business.

SIMON
And presumably talk about his father.

LOUISE
No idea. I don't know how close they were.

SIMON
Her and Jack?

LOUISE
No, her and John. *[Pauses].* I have no idea.

SIMON
Mmm.

LOUISE
Well. *[Sighs.]* He was almost at Camaiore when the traffic stopped. There was a line of cars as far as he could see. It was the Wolf-Man. *[Says this with force].*

[Pause.]

SIMON
The way you say that –

LOUISE
What?

SIMON
You say that, about the Wolf-Man, as though you're frustrated.

LOUISE
I'd have thought it would make more sense trying to find the Wolf-Man than trying to make out I'm a killer.

SIMON
They don't believe you killed those women.

LOUISE
Right. *[Sighs].* Just my best friend and her husband.

[Silence.]

Why would I do that?

SIMON
Maybe you were jealous?

LOUISE
I wasn't jealous.

SIMON
Or perhaps that John had taken Kate from you.

[There's a long silence. A sound of movement.]

LOUISE
Can I stand up?

SIMON *[Warily.]*
Yes.

LOUISE
I don't know what to say to that. *[Measured, quiet.]* You're absolutely fucking stupid. *[Painfully. Sound of footsteps slowly moving from microphone.]* Are you all right with me looking out of the window?

SIMON *[More warily still.]*
Yes.

LOUISE
Just thought I'd check. Nothing else you say makes sense.
What if the fucking Wolf-Man killed John and Kate? What
about that? Why isn't anybody talking about that?

[Silence.]

CHAPTER 6
HARLEY STREET 2010 /
PISA, 1986

The silence stretched on – something distracted me. Kay seemed to be crying. While I was listening I must have had my eyes closed. Now I saw her looking into space, tears running down her cheeks as she sobbed. I didn't say anything. I watched her. The silence continued and Louise spoke.

I touched my face. I'd been crying, too.

Kay closed her eyes; and I closed mine.

*

LOUISE
I didn't kill anybody.

[Footsteps returning. Sounds as though she is sitting down.]

It was the first of the killings: a woman about my age. They found her car in a barn. There was blood on the seats, which were torn up as though a dog had been at them. The windscreen was painted over.

SIMON
What?

LOUISE
You didn't know? The windscreen was sprayed black, from the inside.

SIMON
Yes.

LOUISE
While John was waiting he said he started to think about his father. His father's hands, holding him when he was very little. His father's face a couple of inches away from him. He remembered running his little hands over his father's stubble, looking for shapes in the ceiling, him singing a song. He remembered his father's voice booming, deep so it made his bones shake. He remembered his father's eyes on him, loving him. He remembered how warm his father's body was, what it was like feeling his father breathing on him.

SIMON *[Pause.]*
Breathing? *[Sceptical.]*

LOUISE
Yes, we both knew it wasn't real. That's what terrified him. He was sitting staring at the cars, the heat haze coming off

the roofs, when suddenly he started remembering his father, even though he knew his father never set a hand on him.

[Pause.]

He steered out of the traffic, turned around, headed back towards Pisa, took the first turning he came to, one snaking up into the hills, and he started to cry. He told me he'd never cried like that before.

Eventually he stopped. He couldn't remember how long he'd been driving. He couldn't remember driving at all. He parked, closed his eyes, sat still, opened them after a few seconds and found himself looking at a dusty path heading away from the road.

His portable phone, his *mobile* phone – he was so bloody proud of it – it rang like they do: that electronic tweeting. He looked at the screen and saw the Wasing number.

[Silence and then the sound of breathing becomes distinct. She speaks and it's obvious this is her breathing, quick, excited.]

May I have some more water?

SIMON
Of course. Here ...

[A bottle is opened. The sound of water pouring and then a movement, perhaps Simon reaching out to Louise. The sound of drinking.]

SIMON
When did he tell you this?

73

LOUISE
When he got back from Italy.

SIMON
What you're saying is very detailed.

LOUISE
Detail's important, so I remember it.

SIMON
I use a tape recorder.

[Silence.]

Louise?

[Silence.]

You said John saw Kate's number on his mobile phone. The Wasing number?

LOUISE
Yes. Kate told me what she said when he answered.

SIMON
Kate told you?

LOUISE
When I was at Wasing.

[Silence.]

She rang him from the library and explained about the honeymoon. He sounded too calm, like he wasn't all there, and told her not to worry. So she got angry and snapped at him.

'It's just a hotel,' he said. They could have the honeymoon anywhere they wanted. It didn't matter. He told her they could have it at Wasing if she wanted.

She didn't want it at Wasing.

He said to leave it to him.

She didn't like that. She asked him where he was and he told her he'd found his way somewhere by accident.

'You're lost,' she said.

No, he told her he wasn't lost. He knew where he was. He told her how beautiful it was and that he'd been there before, with his mother.

SIMON
With his mother?

LOUISE
He realised while he was sitting there.

[Pause.]

Kate asked him to describe the place. And he told her what came to him – about walking along the dusty path with his mother, past wild cherry trees and olive trees, holding her hand. He told her about the birds he could see and the sun, and that he was going to take a walk down the track to clear his head. Kate was happier with that. They said goodbye and then ...

SIMON
And then what?

LOUISE
That was when the things at the house happened.

SIMON
Which things?

LOUISE
You must know. It was reported. Some clown leaked it
from my first interview with Semproni.

SIMON
Can you tell me anyway?

LOUISE
No. What I'd like to do is turn this –

[A click: the hiss of silence.]

CHAPTER 7
HARLEY STREET, 2010

Kay had her hand under the scarf she was wearing, stroking her neck. Her gaze was fixed far away.

'She switched her microphone off,' she said.

The hiss continued.

'You think so?'

'I know so.'

The hiss stopped suddenly.

LOUISE
After she finished talking to John ... she was in the library ...

SIMON *[Impatiently.]*
Yes?

LOUISE
There's no clock in the library. No ticking, no paintings. Nothing to remind you life might be going on somewhere else. The curtains are usually drawn and the electric light's switched on even if it's the middle of the day, in the middle of the summer.

SIMON
That's where Kate was when she rang John about her honeymoon being cancelled.

LOUISE
Yes. Usually she loved it in there, shut away where Jack France used to write. All of his books were in his library. Each of *his* books and every one of the books he liked: it was like a nest. All of Robert Browning on a single shelf. His poems and each of his letters.

[Silence]

But that afternoon she wished she was somewhere else. Because when she reached out for a copy of *K* she felt somebody else was there with her.

[She pauses for several seconds.]

SIMON
Who knew what Kate was writing?

LOUISE
What do you mean?

SIMON
Her book, her replies to the letters in *K*.

LOUISE
Only me.

SIMON
Just you. Not John?

LOUISE
No. She started writing it in secret. After you do that there's no going back, really, is there? She told herself that by writing the replies, her own replies, she might get to know more about John.

SIMON
How would that work?

LOUISE
Jack was his father. You can't help having a piece of your father inside you, can you?

[A long silence.]

SIMON
She thought she'd learn about John by writing as if to his father?

LOUISE
There was no as if. He was dead, but she was still writing to him, wasn't she?

SIMON
Not much hope of a reply, though, was there?

LOUISE
Maybe she thought she could learn something without getting that kind of a reply.

SIMON
Maybe.

LOUISE
She was in the library at Wasing and she took down a copy of *K* and opened it – near the end, I would imagine. She had just finished her reply to the ninth letter; it's the one where he writes about becoming a father. He knew he was going to be a father some time before he was married. And there was just the tenth one to go – which is only a couple of pages long.

[Silence.]

SIMON
What did she do?

LOUISE
She opened the book. What happened next was very odd. She described what happened – she described it to me in a lot of detail.

SIMON
Go on.

LOUISE
She called out: *Hello?* She thought there was somebody there. The rooms echo at Wasing. She imagined them echoing all of the way to the main road, across the fields, as though she were shouting out on the edge of a lake.

SIMON
How do you mean?

LOUISE
That echoing noise you get when you speak in a big, old room. She imagined it spilling out of the house, over the fields. That time of year the fields were cut short and they might as well have been water as grass, and the house on an island.

SIMON
Go on.

LOUISE
She felt as though someone was looking at her. *What do you mean?* I asked her. *Like in my dream*, she said. *Something was there but*, she said, *it wasn't quite there.* She had to get out of there before it arrived; she ran to the door, threw it open and slammed it behind her, holding on to the handle so that if something on the other side turned it – she could stop it.

SIMON
If something turned it? *[He sounds appalled, as if listening to something childish].*

LOUISE
And she still had the book with her, the copy of *K*. She thought she could use it like an axe – to chop it down if she had to. She leaned closer to the door, not quite touching it, her ear a couple of inches from the wood, her finger still holding the handle. Something was happening: there was a pumping noise, a muffled thudding. It was her own heart. Then behind her, there was a sigh.

She shrieked and let go of the handle. She was shaking.

SIMON *[Disbelieving.]*
A sigh?

LOUISE
She was going to run out of the front door but the library was at the back of the house. She'd have to go down the hall, and that was dark now, past the living room and the dining room and maybe there'd be ... she called out again: *hello*? Her voice sounded as though it was locked in a tiny box, one you might keep pins in, a little tin. That's how it sounded.

[She pauses, sounds scared. Sound of her breathing.]

She went upstairs.

SIMON
Upstairs? Why would she do that? Didn't she want to get out?

LOUISE
Yes. But she ran upstairs to the bend in the staircase. Whatever it was, she said, it felt like the higher up she got

she'd be getting away from it. It was like a dog following her, whatever it was, as though the book was a piece of meat. She dropped it down the staircase. It landed at the bottom, and the house felt very still. And quiet. She heard her heart again – like there was a party in one of the rooms, the music making the walls throb. But it was quiet. She stared at the book at the bottom of the stairs, its pages splayed, and then at the door to the library.

The door was shut. She backed against the window. Something was going on – she knew … something was happening. There was a scratching. She looked at the library door and listened: a scratching, but not from in there. She thought she might faint – at first. Then she felt brave.

What was scratching?

Mice, she thought. It was mice in a big old country house; and the sigh? Something getting shifted. A bag of something in the kitchen. She imagined the noise of a bag of flour being pushed along one of the old wooden shelves in the larder, there in the damp-smelling, old, vegetably inside of the larder.

It wasn't in the larder though. It wasn't downstairs at all: it was upstairs.

There were mice in the attic. So she took a breath and carried on up the stairs. At the top the noise was louder. It was real. There wasn't any doubt about it: there was a scratching, a scraping coming from one of the rooms along the corridor, towards the one where she and John slept: John's old room. She went towards it.

No, the noise was coming from the next room. A rough, scraping sound.

The door was closed. She waited. The noise continued. It was mice. *What was scratching*? Stupid. What did she think it would be? She turned the handle and pushed open the door. It swung back gently on its hinges – and the musty smell inside wafted out as though she had leaned closer to a flower, an unpleasant one. This one: a fungus.

Inside it was dark.

I was there: me, Christopher, in the dark. Louise's voice was like an echo, like the echo in the room she described Kate hearing: but the first sound, the first movement, the first thing, was me. I am Kate and the curtains are drawn. I'm looking at them, nervously, heavy old velvet things, waiting for one of them to move, as if something could spring at me. I ache – I'm so tense. I can hear my heart all right; it's like music in the next room, the beat of my heart pounding.

This is John's mother's room. I switch on the light. It makes no difference: I am still as scared. There's a wardrobe in front of me, dark cherry red and the door is open. I remember when I was little, going into the box room when we moved in – wasn't that under the place where my father stored his stuff, in the attic, when I cleared it all out?

This is all fucked up. Where am I?

In front of me there's a chocolatey wardrobe and I'm on all fours. How old am I? I'm Kate and I'm a grown woman; I'm Chris and I am ... I'm scared. I am scared. I am scared. This wardrobe, I can't eat it: the door's open. It's chocolatey red and I can't eat it. Look at all her old clothes: old woman's clothes. And a smell of paper: wet raffle tickets.

The cherrywood wardrobe and something flat on the floor in front of it. Like something dead. It's been run over.

I step to the side of it. There's a shawl beside it. What's this? It's a painting, and I've seen that place. I've been there. Kate hasn't though: how can that be? If I'm Kate, and I look down at myself, in my dress – and I have bare feet. Those aren't my feet. Those are Kate's. It's a painting next to my toes. I've painted my nails red.

It's the Villa. There's no tower. Something's scratched it away. Something has scraped at it so there's a space down the middle of the canvas: a stripe torn away by his mother. I know: John's mother did this.

LOUISE
Yes. The tower at the Villa Inghilterra. She picked the canvas up and put it back on the shelf of the wardrobe. Mice, she thought. She shut it away, checked everything else was in order, turned the light off and closed the door. That feeling of being looked at was gone.

CHAPTER 8
HARLEY STREET, 2010 /
PISA, 1986

She opened her eyes. They were still full of tears.

It's you, I wanted to say out of nowhere. What did I mean? I couldn't bear the thought. Something about looking at Kay was unbearable, and I closed my eyes. Louise began to speak again. I listened, I slipped into it. I cut myself off from Kay's tears and pictured what she was saying.

LOUISE
John told me it was dark when he walked back to his car.

I'd seen pictures of John. He was tall, athletic. I imagined him standing talking about his father at the front of the packed lecture theatre, Louise and Kate watching, Jack France and Robert Browning projected behind him on a screen reaching from the floor to the ceiling. John was a fraction of the size of those famous faces, but he still looked strong.

He walked quickly. He'd look around him, something of an animal about him however cultivated he seemed. There had to be if there was any Browning in him. Something of a kind of city fox, more than a bit of a dog. A man who used his instincts. A kind of an animal man who, in his way, could turn heads as much as his father or his however many great-grandfathers Robert.

He was successful. He used his instincts to stock his gallery with the kinds of art that would always be easy to sell. I imagined him talking to Christina, that survivor from his father's world, and still being able to cast his own spell. I thought of him visiting her gallery and standing his ground with her, enchanting her enough for her to remember Jack, at the very least. He was no weak copy of Jack. He'd feel at home with her.

On his way to the villa, while the sun was shining, he said he had a vague sense he was going somewhere he'd been before, when he was very young. He realised that there must have been somebody with him. It was so remote. And he had a sense of somebody tall walking beside him – and other feelings, as if he was reading a book he had read many times before, with its familiar creases, tears and folded page corners. But there were no words.

The tall figure was his mother. He remembered holding her hand, what that was like ... how it didn't feel quite right, quite secure, as though he knew she was worried without her having to say anything; she was holding on to him more tightly than was comfortable. It didn't make sense. Wouldn't he feel safe if she held him tightly? Several steps later, and that was all it took, he knew he didn't want to hold her hand any more. She was moving too quickly, she was holding on too tight, and he didn't trust her. She was stiff. When they walked along their arms should be swinging together, their hands like the pendulum on a big clock.

But she wouldn't let go.

[Louise changes pace, talking more slowly, more deliberately, as if she is really seeing what she is describing.]

She was gone. That had been remembering. At the end of the track there was a villa, almost too beautiful, with walls that seemed to shimmer as the sun set. Beside it, covered in scaffolding and standing alone, maybe fifty feet high, was a stone tower. He sat down on a grassy bank, the grass stiff like bristles, watching it get dark, feeling it get colder.

As it grew darker lights came on. The moon lit the building's pale walls with a mysterious blue light that made its ledges, gutters, chimneys and tiles stand out as if they were strange ornaments. The shadow of the tower was so long it almost reached his feet.

He saw a woman with her hair tied in a knot go into a room on the middle floor – there were three floors – and she changed the linen on a bed. He heard a car approach from the other side of the building and realised there was a road. Headlights briefly dazzled him as the vehicle drove into view and stopped outside the front door. A couple got out with a suitcase. A man approached to help them, an older man who moved slowly.

He took the cases and the couple walked ahead.

A light came on in one of the top floor rooms. Another woman who was naked and beautiful stepped to the window and stood for a second, gazing out towards him, as if she was looking straight through him, far into the hills beyond him. A man appeared at her side, draping his arm over her shoulder and they kissed. She drew the curtains.

The man who had taken the suitcases reappeared from the front door, got into the car and drove it to a low garage with a pitched roof.

It was a hotel. The couple he'd seen were in love. And as that thought came to him so did others, surging forward. All of the thoughts he'd had while he was driving, everything since he'd set foot in Italy, all of it had taken him to that moment in front of that building. He remembered his mother standing in front of him on that same spot. He was a little boy, frightened and cold, sitting on the same grassy bank. She stood with her hands clasped in front of her as she drew as close to the building as she could without attracting the attention of anyone inside. Her shoulders rose and fell as if she was taking sharp breaths. His mother. Before he was sent off to school his life was full of scenes like that: of him lying in bed as a little boy and her climbing the stairs, then tiptoeing to the bottom again, and again, and again, and again; of her looking up into the air and telling him, one day, she'd show him how to catch his dreams; of her talking to herself but hardly ever to other people. None of it made sense, although at the time, with just the two of them together, of course it did. Why not?

He listened carefully and heard the sound of crickets, somewhere he heard the wind in the trees.

It was a hotel. The one where his father had disappeared.

[Silence]

I want to stop.

[Uncomfortable. There's the sound of movement, a click, a hiss of static. The recording stops. And then there's Simon's voice.]

SIMON

Joan, I need to tell you, these Italians have no idea how to make a cup of tea. I spent half an hour this morning arguing the toss over the fact this place seems addicted to the bloody teabag. And I had such high hopes ... yesterday morning wasn't bad at all. But these continentals, they have an intrinsic stubbornness Chris would be proud of. Whoops. Strike that. Any luck though and I'll be out of here tomorrow; if not, I think you'll need to find me somewhere else. Coffee, fine. But you ask for a fucking cup of tea and it's like trying to – OK, better not go there. Chris: if you're listening, that earlier comment was a joke. That's J.O.K.E. You are the least stubborn man I know.

[Slowly, sarcastically, then laughs to himself.]

Anyway, am I getting anywhere with the Signorina Louise? Yes, maybe, possibly, perhaps. She *is* an irritating little thing. Can you log the fact that she continues to fantasise, I imagine as a way of defending herself from the thought she somehow disposed of her best friend. I am hearing stories about John France's mother and father, about Kate getting spooked in that mansion of theirs, Wasing, about letter-writing projects, about Oxford. Oh Lord. Perhaps tomorrow we'll get to what happened once the happy couple got as far as Tuscany. Can you imagine, having your honeymoon at the same place where your father vanished? Oh might I ask you, when you have a minute, but perhaps rather sooner than later, if you could rustle up a couple of tickets for the Lord's Test?

[A click. A hiss: blank tape.]

CHAPTER 9
HARLEY STREET, 2010

As the tape hissed I became aware Kay was looking at me. There was a looseness in her expression, a gentleness. I didn't say anything.

She spoke to me. 'You look like you're a long, long way off.'

The candles flickered.

'It didn't feel like it.'

Snow blew against the window like confetti that would never melt.

'Do you believe her?' she asked.

'Do I believe what?'

'He's trying to undermine her.'

'I've told you what I think of Simon.'

'But you still keep in touch with him.'

'That doesn't mean anything. I don't think she killed anybody. No. It doesn't mean anything that I'm in touch with Simon.'

'Doesn't it?' She flicked her hair out of her eyes. 'Perhaps the moment Simon realises you object to the way he does things will be the moment he does things differently.'

The tape hissed.

'I don't think so.'

'Perhaps it will be the point when you stop speaking.'

'I don't speak to Simon any more.' There was a click. The cassette player stopped and a red light blinked.

Kay shook her head. 'I think the batteries are flat.'

CHAPTER 10
PISA, 1986

LOUISE
I've lost the thread.

[*There's a strange silence, as if someone has forgotten their lines. As if someone's read the script wrongly.*]

LOUISE
I think I might stop here. I don't want to say anything else.

SIMON
You haven't said anything yet today.

LOUISE
No.

SIMON
We need to go on.

LOUISE
No.

[Whispers something, as if to herself.]

CHAPTER 11
HARLEY STREET, 2010

Something was different. I wanted to keep listening, but Kay was looking around us as if there was something else on her mind.

'You want to keep listening?' she asked. 'We'll need some batteries if you do.'

I thought about my desk. There weren't any there.

'I'm cold.' She reached for her coat, slipped it on and buttoned it up to her neck. 'And I'm very tired.'

I told her, without really thinking, that there was a couch in my consulting room she could lie down on. It felt wrong as soon as I said it.

She frowned: 'I don't think so.'

'I can look downstairs for some batteries.' I felt dazed, as if I'd been sleeping and had just woken up, as though I'd been dreaming. I stood up, determined to bring myself back into the present. I thought of the receptionist's desk and some of the other rooms down there that I knew were never locked: the waiting room everybody who occupied the building shared, and the basement where the recycling bins were stored – cardboard, plastic – by the end of each week it was full of rubbish that couldn't go in the bins.

'You go,' she said.

'You sure?'

She touched her scarf and nodded.

I picked up the candle which seemed to have the tallest flame and made my way out into the stairwell.

It was colder out there, far colder. The staircase spiralled down below me, my candle illuminating far more than I'd imagined, casting great, soft shadows. I descended into the silence, one step at a time, the smell of wax all around me.

I tilted the candle so the wax wouldn't run onto my fingers and raised it above my head as I reached the ground floor. Apart from the desk by the entrance there was no other furniture and, although the surface of the desk was lit evenly, everything below it was almost dark. Outside I heard the wind. The front door rattled as a gust blew and the tiny figures, a reindeer and an angel, dangling from the little Christmas tree on the desk, shivered like the flame.

I tried both of the desk drawers. They were empty.

So, there was the waiting room, but the door to that was shut. I tried the handle and felt the latch lift. The door groaned as I opened it and inside it was colder still. Colder, and completely dark. I'd only ever been inside during daylight, when it was possibly the brightest room in the building. Now my candle showed me an iron shutter drawn over the French windows onto the small courtyard I sometimes peered down into, leaning from the window in my consulting room, when I wanted to feel the sun on my face.

I don't like the dark.

I stepped into the room and approached a heavy-looking mahogany chest next to the fireplace, my footsteps clicking on the parquet, the candlelight playing on the sombre paintings and the old books in the cabinets. If I lowered the candle, the shadows shifted all around me. The door swung shut behind me.

'Hello?' I called out without thinking, and I felt foolish. I thought of Kate, in the library at Wasing. The silence weighed on me. A drop of wax fell from the tip of the candle and landed on the parquet blocks. I dragged my feet over it, still without thinking, and smeared a grey streak on the floor. I *was* stupid.

Why was I so nervous?

I returned to the door and opened it, and closed it again. Opened it, and closed it. And I did it again. The third time I felt better. I told myself to stop wasting time.

The cabinet was locked. I tried every drawer. Where else could I look? There was the basement.

I laughed to myself and felt a prickle down my neck.

There was only one way to do it. I went back to the door, pulled it open, walked to the end of the hall, covering the flame with my hand, carried on straight down the short series of steps to the basement, through the heavy modern door at the bottom – and then I stopped. I stared.

Still protecting the flame with my hand, the enormous shadows of my fingers fell across the scene in front of me: two rows of plastic bins, chest-high, each full to the brim with waste paper and plastic. The place, a narrow, horrible little room that must have once held coal, or wood, smelled of damp cardboard. Nobody could have lived there, with its nasty mildewed walls. At the far end there was an impenetrable-looking door to the outside. And suddenly, standing there, I felt like a boy wandering into the middle of a wood, who's heard a branch crack behind him, an animal cry out close to him. And it was all I could do to not to turn on my heels and run.

Wolves.

Below me – and I can't believe the sense of it which suddenly swallowed me up – there was earth, cold earth. Above me, way above me, there was a thick layer of snow on the roof. I felt so small, and utterly alone.

Angry for allowing myself that thought, I stared around hatefully for the thing I'd set myself to get. And I grew more angry, knowing that what I was doing was purely so I could listen to her.

Who was Kay? I grasped at the strangeness of it, maybe feeling it for the first time. Who was she? The woman in my office, Kay, this woman who'd had me invite Louise back into my life after so many years when I hadn't remembered her once?

There were no cupboards down there, only shelves above the bins, then down in the shadows on the floor I noticed a transistor radio. I picked it up. There wasn't any flex; no plug. I switched it on and a serious voice, tinny, all treble, addressed the room about something that seemed utterly unimportant. I looked at my watch and saw it was just after the hour.

I switched it off again, hoping its batteries would be the same as those in the cassette player. I realised I hadn't even checked to see what kind of batteries I needed. Well I had what I had.

I backed up towards the steps, letting the door swing shut. The latch clicked into place, but before I even had time to turn around a draught hit me. My flame danced hopelessly and died. The front door slammed.

In the darkness I scrambled to the top of the steps and saw a faint, pale line which I guessed marked some form of light creeping in from the street – and the glow of another candle sitting on the receptionist's desk. One from my room: Kay's.

'Is anyone there?'

I put my candle down, its waxy smell filling the hall.

'Hello?'

I ran to the door, grabbed the handle and threw it open. The force of the freezing wind caught me as if someone was shoving with icy hands. The candle flame was nearly annihilated, but clung onto the wick, just. Snow gusted in around my feet. I looked out, my eyes screwed up. There was nobody there. I called out but no one replied. There were footsteps in the snow, a few that looked fresh. What was I supposed to do? She'd gone – Kay, it must have been her. I could have followed but why should I have followed, not even certain that she'd gone?

I picked her candle up, a shorter, fatter one with a stronger flame and opened the door to the waiting room. It was empty, the shutters still fastened, the wax from my candle still streaking the floor. I went back to the receptionist's desk, looked underneath it – nothing.

I went back to my rooms and searched them. I searched all of the rooms: my consulting room, even the lavatory, the cloakroom, and finally the group room. A circle of eight empty chairs stood in the middle of an old Afghan rug. She was gone.

I looked for a note, for any sign she'd been there at all. There was absolutely nothing, apart from the candle that I held in my hand. I opened up the back of the radio and pulled out the batteries. They fitted. Feeling restless I looked out of the window and saw that the street was empty.

I locked the door onto the landing and poured myself a glass of water. I switched the cassette player back on and rewound a little, back to where Louise mentioned John going to see Christina. How could he have found the Villa Inghilterra like that? It sounded far-fetched. How could John have stumbled on the hotel where his father had vanished? I pressed play. Louise spoke almost immediately, but as if there'd been a break with what I'd already heard.

LOUISE
He drove to Camaiore. *[Pauses, as if she's thinking.]* Like he'd meant to do the afternoon before, after he arrived in Pisa.

[Silence.]

I remember, when I went there was a clump of tents in a field on the outskirts of the town, a few policemen walking around, smoking, not saying much, looking unhappy.

[Sounds back inside the story, all dreamy.]

SIMON
When you went?

LOUISE *[Restlessly.]*
Yes, you know, when I went. After John disappeared. When Kate got in touch with me. *[Pause.]* I saw some men pacing in the olive trees in the next field, walking around in circles. You know the way those trees look in the sun, huddled

over the little patches of earth underneath them. They look pretty desperate.

[Silence.]

Do you know Camaiore?

SIMON
No.

LOUISE
You drive through Pisa along the coast for an hour or so, you drive through those tolls they have on the motorway, the *autostrade*, and then you wind down some loops and runs through little towns. There are warehouses, odd places, modern ones, great cubes with flat roofs and pipes sticking out of the sides.

I got lost and ended up in an industrial park. It was deserted, run down, but new, as if it had barely been used, as though it had been built to fall apart.

If you get as far as Camaiore, the chances are you'll still miss it. It isn't small, but it's so out of the way, in the Alps, The *Alpi Apuane*. It is beautiful. There's an abbey.

John was going to see Christina at her gallery.

SIMON
Why would he want to do that?

LOUISE
To find out about the place he'd ended up at the day before.

SIMON
So what did she say?

[A long pause.]

LOUISE
You're impatient.

[Another pause, this one his. It's longer, but it would be.]

SIMON
What did she say?

[A short silence.]

LOUISE
Christina recognised the building... he'd seen and told him where to find it. It was called the Villa Inghilterra.

SIMON
I thought he knew where it was.

LOUISE
No. He got there by accident. *[Another pause.]* After he saw Christina he drove there. In the daylight. *[Pause.]*
The villa's impressive. There's nothing else around it. It looks a lot bigger than it would with other houses around it – monumental. When you get there the first thing that strikes you isn't the villa, though, but the tower beside it. It's covered in scaffolding and a tarpaulin wrapped around the top, a red one. It looks a little like a huge match. And that's where John's parents spent their honeymoon.

I remember standing there thinking that, while the couple who owned it, the Smiths, came towards me. They wondered who I was. Kate's friend. Maybe I'd know what to do. A corner of the tarpaulin flapped. There was a breeze up there. Not on the ground.

I asked them about the tower at some point that evening. I wondered what had happened to it. Mr Smith told me it was a clock tower, a clockless tower. The previous owner had sold the clock: the face, the hands, the mechanism.

Inside the villa – all the oak panelling came from England. There's a set of double doors with Cupids carved into them. The honeymoon suite. *Luna di miele. Viaggio di nozze ...*

Louise was rambling. She talked more about her journey there, about travelling, and my mind turned to the times my family travelled to Scotland when I was a child. I looked towards the window, slightly misted now. The room was cooler with the heater off – getting cold, and with it there was that sense of somewhere abandoned. I didn't like it.

I thought about the cottage we went to every year when I was a child, which stood empty most of the time. I thought how cold that little place became every winter, miles from anywhere else – granite blocks for walls that kept out the cold if you lit a fire but kept it in, like a tomb, if the place was deserted. I thought of that place, cold in the winter, because somehow it reminded me of my father. At the time I'd thought it was a happy place, a refuge. Each year after we stopped going there, though, those happy memories grew fainter.

I thought of the summer.

Every summer, sometimes each Easter, we'd head north to spend the school holidays at the cottage. There were a lot of us: my mother, my three sisters and my brother. A dog, and an *au pair*. My father travelled up with us and then returned to London as quickly as he could – to see his girlfriends; to keep an eye on his dodgy businesses.

If we caught the train, Dad would step out onto the station platform at Perth, a couple of stops south of Aberdeen. We'd ask where he was going, us older children at any rate. My younger brother and sister were probably just as aware there was something odd about the way he, normally bullish, pushy, noisy and angry, grew quieter as the train approached Perth. He became pale and tense. Eventually he'd stand in the corridor, looking away from us, and Mum would take something out of the big cloth bag she carried with her: a game for us to play, a comic for each of us. Some sweets. Once I remember Mum dropped the bag and we all shouted out at once. Dad turned around and there were tears in his eyes. I wondered what was going on. I asked Mum, but as usual she said that Dad liked to step out and get a breath of the Perth fresh air. If he liked the air so much, I remember thinking, why was he acting so strangely?

A few years later, when we were poorer after Dad's business started to go bust, we started to drive rather than take the train. How much would it have cost, taking five children, a dog, an *au pair* and two adults to Scotland? Don't ask how we all fitted into one car, even if it was a Volvo estate, a red one that smelled enduringly like a new car long after it started to rust. So we drove. For some reason holidays were essential – some archaic thought, perhaps, of departing from the city for the summer. My father came from a distinguished Polish family. His father had been born in 1858, the same year Darwin was describing evolution.

We drove, and although after Edinburgh it would have been faster to go up the east coast to Aberdeen we detoured inland. To Perth.

At Perth we got lost. Either we'd miss a turning in the city itself and go backwards and forwards over the bridge, during rush hour, until my mother worked out where to turn from her AA map, Swipe whining and a child crying; or we'd make it through the city and miss the turning after Scone Palace.

My father was always driving: my father who never got lost. He couldn't get out of Perth though. Each year there was the ritual: the return to Perth like a great beast returning to a watering hole. Did I ever ask my mother why? I don't think any of us did. There seemed too much at stake. A wrong word about Perth might drive Dad over the line, into the steaming, screaming rages that still terrify me, even as distant memories. No wonder I can sometimes only laugh at them. I flatten them out like cartoons and search for speech bubbles, like the ones I was addicted to in my Tintin books, where I sought refuge from his moods and his madness. There were few words to accompany the cryptic scenes I so regularly found myself in as a child – *woah*. That's a dog. *Blistering Barnacles*. That's a sailor.

Something about Tintin never makes sense even if as a child you manage to understand it. That's what it was like for me.

I only began to understand my father's returning to Perth when I found out he had been imprisoned there for several years. The newspapers described the trial and his terrible, violent crimes. Even then, there wasn't an explanation. Only the information: he'd been locked up, a foreigner in a Scottish jail, straight after the war. It hadn't been fair, my mother told me. He was innocent. I didn't believe her, and I still didn't believe it after he was finally pardoned – it was a couple of years before he died. I read the appeal court's summing up: Dad suffered a mistrial. They didn't say he was innocent.

You know how innocent someone is if you live with them long enough.

Guilty, I thought, as the tape of Louise speaking came to an end.

Guilty fucker. He was guilty.

The tape finished. I didn't want to spend another minute in there. I thought of the model tower in the next room. I thought of my father, and it sent me off into the snow.

CHAPTER 12
HARLEY STREET, 2010

I buttoned my coat as I headed down the stairs. I couldn't get out of there quick enough. I needed speed before I passed that desk with its little Christmas tree. I swung my bag, helping me gather momentum, turned each corner with a lurch and, when I got to the bottom, I don't think I even looked at the desk. I was out of the door and into the street, snow halfway up my calves before I could stop myself. God, it was cold. I took a few crunching, staggering steps. The street lights lit the length of Harley Street better than if it were a film set: a long white streamer heading up towards Regent's Park, traffic lights blinking here and there; nothing else moving. Just me and the traffic lights.

I kept moving, aware of an awfulness in each step, one that had more in common with striding out into a cold sea off the south coast in summer, the water rising towards my waist, than that of a man stepping into the snow which had paralysed London. It felt funny, exciting – but there, at the very edge of my awareness, was the fear of something truly frightening: people died doing things like this. People die wading off the beach and people die in the snow.

Where was I heading?

The Langham. Why not? Two minutes' walk ordinarily: it took me ten. A young man at the desk watched as I stood in the doorway brushing snow from my trousers, a doorman holding my bag. They had a room – plenty of rooms. It seemed I was one of the only people in London who hadn't known there was a blizzard coming.

I tried to remember what had been on my mind when I woke that morning which had left me so oblivious. I took my train as usual from Canterbury, leaving at six-fifty. It had crawled to Ashford like it generally did, the same people as ever on board. Then? I'd read for the rest of the journey, all the way from Ashford to St Pancras. Normally I took as little notice as possible of Ashford, beyond an occasional thrill at all the foot-high lights scattered around the track outside the station.

But had I been reading? I'd been thinking. I saw it now, the book in my hands, something by Carl Hiaasen, but I hadn't been reading. I'd been dreaming about the view out of my new consulting room windows. What it would be like to look out onto Regent's Park? All that grass. The trees. All those people.

When I reached St Pancras I got off the train and stood on the platform, listening to the cricket score from Australia; and, as I remembered, the platform was almost empty. Usually you wouldn't be able to stand there like that. I'd been almost on my own – in my head and then in the world. I recalled how empty the train had been. How different the streets had been as I walked to Harley Street: nobody crossing my path, glancing at me as they approached and changing direction. The shops – had they been open? I didn't know. I hadn't noticed.

So I was at the Langham and that, too, was half empty. I went up to my room, number eleven, all alone in the lift and walked down a corridor feeling sealed-in, slightly sickened. There was a sort of stale warmth, a dry overheating. However plush a hotel feels it seems cheap to me if its windows don't open. As I approached my room I noticed all of these things, hyper-aware, maybe, after considering my deadened state that morning. It didn't set me up well, that's for sure. I would be warm that night but I could also be asphyxiated by corporate cling film. Too much worry about fire and safety regulations; not enough about what it feels like lying in something like a Tupperware box.

With the door open, and the light inside off, room eleven looked like a cave. The curtains with their folds looked like a wall of grey rock, floor to ceiling. I put the light on, threw my bag down on the bed, and stared at a picture of a flat landscape, willowy trees obscured by reflections from the main light: where was that? Nowhere, I could be sure. What was I doing there? I looked at my bag: carelessness. Wasn't that how I ended up in Italy, with Louise?

I put my hand in my bag and took out the tapes in their sharp-edged plastic cases. There was my tape recorder, too. How horribly familiar. It wasn't the first time I'd been in a hotel room with those tapes, no.

I wanted a drink – but something soft. Nothing that would tamper with my brain any more than the afternoon already had.

I took the second tape out of its case, the one with my handwriting on it, and thought about listening to it. I sat down on the bed, full of feeling, leaning forward with my head between my knees. I rocked.

I could remember setting up the recording to make that tape: the Italian guard trying to tell me the best place to put my microphone. Such a clear memory. That dog of a man picking up my cassette player and holding onto it like it was his.

'Over here,' he said. 'Best place.' How I detested his broken, shitty English. There'd been a small table next to the chair where Louise was about to sit and that, in his opinion, was where the tape needed to go.

'No,' I told him. 'Here's better.' I wanted to pull the table to the middle of the room.

'Why here?' he asked, staring at the place on the floor I'd indicated as if I'd just shat there.

'It's in the middle.'

'Before, he have it here.' *Before* – he meant with Simon.

'I want it placed equally between myself and Miss Finnegan.'

'Why?'

This went on until I let him have his way. After he left the room I put the table where I wanted it, the tape recorder on top and ... I waited.

No, I didn't want to listen to the tape then. It could wait.

I left my things on the bed and went down to one of the bars. I ordered a coffee and sat in a corner, a scattering of people around me, most of them in pairs. It felt pretty easy and I started to relax, reading a newspaper.

There on the front page: SNOW CHAOS. So I missed it. Big deal. I could sit there a while, I thought, get myself together, then maybe listen to the tape; maybe not.

I must have been reading for fifteen or twenty minutes when I became aware of someone approaching. People had come and gone around me the whole time I'd been sitting there and, while I might have noticed them, I only barely did. It was like being in bed, a window open so the curtain occasionally shifts in the night breeze. But when that person walked by it was as if that curtain had lifted up; and when a curtain does that you look. Something might be out there; something may have happened.

I lowered my newspaper.

'Hi.' Kay smiled down at me. 'What a surprise.' She'd removed her scarf. Her fingers went to a little golden book on a chain around her neck, open as if lying on a lectern. I'd seen one of them before, those little book necklaces. I couldn't remember where.

I caught the scent of something, a perfume I half-recognised. She was wearing a black dress but a different one. This one had long sleeves that clung to her arm. There was a pale V from her neck, her skin. I stared at her. She stared at me.

'Well,' she said.

'Where did you go?'

'Can I sit down?' She didn't move – she didn't look worried. She was so still and her stillness was unbearably beautiful, like a moment from a film. A film still: black and white, colour – both together.

I realised I hadn't answered. 'Of course. Please.' She sat opposite me, looked down and then slowly up. 'I need to apologise.'

'Huh?' I was lost.

'For leaving you like that. It was very kind of you to invite me in.'

'It wasn't any trouble for me.' Maybe it was because we'd been at my practice before, my clinic, that I hadn't realised how beautiful she was. How there was something electric about her.

'My curiosity,' she said. 'That was the trouble. I shouldn't have asked you to play the tape.'

A waiter came across. She ordered a glass of wine but no food. I waited as she spoke to him, watching her – watching him. He seemed mesmerised. I thought about how she'd caught my eye, in the street. There were many ways I might not have noticed. After she ordered her wine the waiter continued to stand there.

'That's all,' she said.

'That's all?' He blushed, glancing at me, then at her, and around us. 'I'm sorry,' he said. 'I was ...' His voice trailed off. He shook his head.

'It's been a long day,' she said.

'Yes,' he replied, accepting the excuse she had offered him.

'It was up to me whether or not we played the tape,' I told her.

'Maybe,' she said. 'I can be persuasive.'

'Perhaps,' I said. 'The tapes were already out.'

'They were.'

The waiter placed a glass of red wine on the table.

'Thank you,' she said.

He nodded and left, quickly.

'So why are you here?' she asked.

'Same reason as you, I imagine. The snow.'

'The snow.'

The window beside our table looked down onto Langham Place, as white as a wedding cake.

'We looked out of the window in your room,' she said, sipping her wine. 'You're not just here for a meal?'

'No.'

'You have a room here?' she put her wine glass down.

'Yes.'

'Shall we go there?'

We did. We slept together and I dreamed.

*

In the dream I needed to get into room eleven. It was a place you couldn't find unless you were lucky – but I was. By chance I was in room eleven, and the lights were switched on even though the light should have been coming from the candles in the middle of the room. The candles didn't have a flame, only light. They were Jewish candles: a menorah.

I knew this, but I didn't seem to know how. I wasn't Jewish, and it was something like Christmas – some sort of festival. I didn't know. I was sitting on a sofa, the kind you'd find in a public place like a bar, or a club. Not just any sort of club: somewhere really sleazy. Maybe a brothel. It was most likely a brothel: there were beautiful, naked women in there, coming and going, only wearing furs. It felt like a fashion show but I was on display. They paraded around me, looking at me, as if they were making their minds up about something. One woman was wearing a wolf fur. The wolf's face hung down over one of her breasts and blinked at me.

I said to her: what am I doing here?

She came across, and the other women disappeared. I recognised her without knowing who she was. I knew her face, and her hands. She put her hands on my chest as she leaned down towards me. She moved as close as she could and the fur slipped from her shoulders, landing across my back. I realised I wasn't dressed, but I wasn't naked either. I didn't seem to have a body you could look at: just one that was there. And as the fur fell from her I saw she was wearing a necklace with a little book on it.

'Who are you?' I asked her. She was pressing her hips against the side of my face, like an animal who wanted to get warm. 'I know you, don't I?'

She sat down beside me, took my hand and put it between her legs. She pushed my fingers against her and shifted, as if there was a breeze. Her skin seemed to tighten. She smiled.

'I'm K,' she said. 'K the letter.'

'Not Kay?'

'No, not Kay.' The difference sank in. Of course it was K, not Kay. Her hair was red – a particular red, like sunsets, I thought.

She nodded.

I asked her: 'What's this about?' We were alone and the lights were dimming; really, a sunset. The candles were flickering now. She reached to my shoulders and arranged the fur, so it hung on me like a second skin.

She put her mouth to my ear and whispered, warm and soft. 'I can't say.'

There was somebody else in the room – I knew even though I couldn't see them. And then I did, I saw her: a woman who looked just like K but with skin even whiter and with black hair. The second woman stood back against the wall, giving us as much space as she could, but she couldn't just go – I knew that.

I whispered to K: 'Who are you?'

'I don't know,' she said. 'Ghosts arrive,' she said, standing up again. 'We come without remembering, and without knowing. All we have are our instincts. We have ghost-instincts.' Her lips weren't moving. She touched the book on her necklace again. 'This is a book: the book of you.'

'So you know about me?'

She shrugged. 'No.'

I was confused. 'What do you know?'

'My name,' she said. 'I'm K.'

'K. Why are you called K?'

'I took it from you. Don't you remember thinking it, just before you saw me through the window?'

I tried to remember.

'You don't? You were thinking K. You were thinking about the eleventh letter: K. I called myself Kay.'

'I don't know why you're here.'

'You decided to move. You decided to move so you would find the tapes. You needed to find the tapes because there's something you have still got to do.'

'Which is what?'

'It's your great unknown.' She reached across the table and touched the back of my hand. 'I'm here to help you find your great unknown.'

But the other woman was beside her, the one with dark hair. She took her hand and led her away. K went without looking back. They left me alone, and the light kept getting dimmer – the air, heavier, as if there was going to be a storm. I wanted to get up, but I couldn't find the energy. Room eleven seemed to be the right place even though it was getting darker, and I was on my own, and I started to feel frightened, because that room was a cave and I knew something else had found itself there. Something or somebody who needed a place in the world, someone chased out. There was a flash, like lightning – or a camera flash. I heard the click of a shutter. Someone else had come into the room: somebody smaller than K; someone, a woman, who reminded me of K but who looked younger.

I realised, though, how young I looked. I saw myself in a mirror I hadn't noticed: not all of me, but part of me. The side of my face, my ear, my jaw, my eye. This was my face of twenty-five years ago and the woman in the room looked not much younger than me. I found myself looking at her neck. She had a necklace but no book. The necklace had a knot – it had been tied, as if it had been snapped. I knew it had been snapped, like her neck. There was the line of what happened on her neck: a white scar.

Her fingers were burned. 'I was holding the wheel,' she said.

'Who?'

'Maria?' she said. She showed me her wrist. 'Look.' There was a tattoo. A number: 110011. 'Concentrate,' she said. 'Concentrate.' The look in her eyes – it was mine. I looked more deeply, telescoping back into a life that wasn't mine and, although I was aware it was a dream – yes, I knew I was dreaming – I also knew I was with someone else, and I felt the weight of the canopy of my father's attic, and the boxes, and the feeling of his cats running around me, moving like flies. I heard the word she was mouthing, because she, like K, was whispering in my ear now – only her breath was cold, like the air over a stream in winter. She whispered the name of a place I can't say. I know the name as much as you, but it wasn't to be said after it was told to me like that. It was told me by someone who had known it.

She showed me her wrist again: 110011. She whispered: 'Room eleven. Nothing in room eleven.'

'Nothing,' I said.

'No, nothing because I am dead.'

'You're a ghost.'

'No, I am dead.' She pursed her lips and blew at me.

*

I woke as if I had been scalded, sitting up before I knew where I was. I looked about me. The room was familiar, but less than where I had been.

Kay touched my arm. 'What is it?' She sounded sleepy.

'Where am I?'

'At the Langham.' The way she said it – it was as if she didn't know what she was committing herself to. 'Chris?'

'I was dreaming.'

'You're sweating.'

'It was a bad dream.'

The curtains weren't drawn. Green light shone through the window.

'It's a Christmas tree,' she said.

A tree? I didn't say anything.

'There are green lights on the tree on the roof of the BBC building.'

I hadn't realised how high up we were.

'Where are the tapes?' she asked.

'On the floor.' I'd thrown the stuff off the bed when we got back to the room.

I reached down, caught hold of the strap to my bag and dragged it up beside me. 'Here.'

'Where did we listen to?' she asked.

'Can we listen to something else?'

'What?'

'The beginning of the second tape. The one I recorded.'

'OK.'

I took out the tape recorder, balanced it on my stomach, changed the tapes and pressed play.

CHAPTER 13
PISA, 1986 / LANGHAM, 2010

After a few moments I heard myself speaking.

'My name's Christopher Katiwa.' I sounded so much younger. That was August 1986. I was listening to a tape recording from nearly twenty-five years ago – in my study, cut off from the world by snow.

Louise replied. 'Doctor *Kateeva*. I wondered how you pronounced it.'

'Chris.'

And I remembered how she looked, sitting opposite me in that strange, shadowy, cluttered room at the police building in Pisa. I remembered her blue eyes, then her heart-shaped face and her dark hair; her arms, folded in her lap, and her legs, which were crossed, and her black shoes with their sharp heels. She sat opposite me, on the verge of a smile, a few strands of hair across her face. I noticed the smell of her perfume, which was something musky and European, not at all English, and the way her skirt folded over her knee. I remembered the suit she was wearing, probably Chanel and the way it fitted perfectly, the jacket unbuttoned, and her silver-grey shirt.

'My blood hurts.'

'Your blood hurts?'

'Yes.'

What could I say?

'I don't see why I have to go through everything again.' The smile, whatever there'd been of it, was gone and she looked tired.

'You don't have to.'

She closed her eyes and opened them slowly. I imagined her counting to ten. 'Simon said that.'

I nodded.

She looked at her hands, slowly moving her fingers. 'He was good at saying nothing, too.'

'But you spoke to him.'

She stared at me. 'Did you say *Chris*?' She waited, as if she wanted to see what I'd do.

I felt my skin prickle. 'Yes, Chris.' She was moving at a different pace from me.

'*Chris*.' She said it with an Italian accent. 'Are you Italian?'

I told her I was English.

'Chris.' She looked surprised and glanced towards the window. 'Chris. How funny, I could have sworn there's something foreign about you. What's going on with your name?'

'My father was Polish.'

She stretched her arms in front of her, clasping then letting go of her wrists, extending her fingers. 'I knew it.' She relaxed, letting her arms fall. 'Can you get me out of here?' She looked away before I could reply. 'No ... How old are you? You look very young.'

'Thirty,' I said. I remembered, as I listened to the tape, how young I had felt.

'Are you experienced?'

I was young, but she couldn't have been much older than me. I'd just finished my training and I wasn't about to get into that. Simon was older and more confident, with a reputation. He had no idea that I'd gone behind his back – gone to Pisa. He was on holiday, his job done, somewhere on the other side of the world.

'I want to help you.'

She laughed. 'Simon didn't go *that* far.'

'No?'

'No. He gave me the impression I was beyond help. He thinks I killed Kate, doesn't he? He thinks I killed John.'

I didn't reply. Silence, I thought. Silence was better. She waved her hand, as if she was used to it.

'My solicitor told me that's what he thinks.'

She shrugged, closed her eyes, tapped her foot, and opened her eyes again, wide, inviting me to look into them. 'You're still here?'

'Your solicitor asked me to speak to you.'

'So?'

'I asked him not to say anything to you before I saw you.'

'Because?'

'I didn't want you to know I was coming in case something got in the way.' I hesitated with what I was about to say. 'I don't think you killed anybody.'

She smiled.

'I don't know what happened, but I don't think you're a killer.'

She shrugged again. 'I didn't.' She paused and glanced at me as if we were sharing a joke. 'What makes you think I didn't?'

I shifted. She raised her eyebrows enough to let me know she'd noticed.

'I don't know.'

She looked at the floor. 'You don't know.' It felt as if she was slipping away.

'No. I don't.' The space between us was unravelling, the tension slackening.

'Why not?'

I told her: 'Your story sounds like a ghost story.'

More distance, as if the ground between us was going to open up. Nothing would cover it. 'Do you believe in ghosts?'

'No.'

'Neither do I,' she said.

'Then why did it sound as if you were telling Simon a ghost story?'

'It's how it happened.' She went over to the window and looked down onto the police vehicles in the courtyard, their roof-lights glittering in the sun. There was something in that look, a kind of intention, which I couldn't work out.

I looked around me, at the piles of old police files and junk stacked along the walls: newspaper, two pairs of boots, a cardboard box, a painting of a white cat with elaborate whiskers. We were talking somewhere that had once been the dining room of a Renaissance villa. Now it was paintingless, chandelierless, tableless ...

If I glanced at all that stuff around us then back at Louise, it felt as if I only had to blink and all the old furniture would fall back into place. The junk would be gone. The trailing cable hanging from the ceiling with its two bare leads, nasty-looking strands of copper wire, would grow a glass chandelier with candles.

'I thought about lying,' she said. 'Some of the things I said to Simon, if I said them again, I'd say them differently. But I didn't lie.'

'You were in Florence.'

'I was working. It was planned weeks before. I went there after the wedding at Wasing.'

'But you were in Florence, what, a couple of hours away?'

'I spent all of my time in the library there – right until the moment Kate called me. Then I went to see her. And yes, it only took a couple of hours.'

I replied quietly. 'I need to be completely clear with you. If you keep saying what you're saying, then they'll find you guilty.'

She stared at me long enough for us to grow old, die, be buried, or burned, cast away, dust. My mind was drifting – I brought myself back.

'Do you want me to start lying?'

'Talk to me.'

'Really?'

'See what happens.'

'See what happens?'

'Will you think about it?'

'Perhaps,' she replied. 'Not now, though.'

'Will you see me again?'

'Tomorrow,' she said. 'Now go away.' She wasn't even looking at me.

I nodded, hesitated, then rang the little bell, a cowbell on a leather strap; a strange arrangement I'd been presented with to call the guard outside the room when I wanted to leave.

'That thing's ridiculous,' she said. 'That bell.'

It was. I ended our first interview with a cowbell.

*

I stopped the tape. Kay touched my arm again.

'You went to Italy.'

I nodded.

'What happened?'

I didn't say anything.

She stroked the back of my hand. 'You don't want to listen to any more?'

'I don't know.'

'We don't have to.'

'That's what you said in Harley Street.'

'Maybe just tell me what happened?'

'It isn't on the tape. There was another interview. Most of what happened – it wasn't on the tape.'

'What did you think Semproni was like?'

'Semproni?' I realised I'd been thinking about him.

'The detective,' she said. 'Simon and Louise mentioned him on the other tape. What was he like?'

'Semproni? I went to see him after the session we just listened to. He smoked a lot.' I remembered his dark eyes. The way he held a cigarette. I went to his office, sat down, and he said to me: *the screws are loose*. He meant the chair. The moment I sat down it sank to one side. I stopped, thinking about it. 'I didn't laugh. He apologised.'

'Go on,' she said. 'What happened?'

'He suggested we swap chairs. I told him it was OK. He gave me a look.'

'How do you mean?'

'I think he was trying to make me feel uncomfortable. He wanted to show me who was in charge.'

'Really.'

'I don't know. He apologised for his room. There was a strip-light, a narrow window.' I could picture it. 'A dented metal window sill. I remember he lifted his hands, looked around us and made a face.

'"She gets the best room in the house," he said. His English was pretty good. "And I get this. They say they're going to do the other building up properly for us," he said, "the villa. They've been saying that ever since I got here, and that was seven years ago."

'I thanked him for agreeing to see me.

'He told me: "Not at all." He said he'd enjoyed meeting Simon, but it didn't sound sincere. Maybe he did that deliberately. I remember he waited for me to pick up the conversation.

'I said I was grateful he'd agreed to let me to speak to Louise. He slapped his hands down on the table.

'"Apparently, according to your colleague, she isn't mad, but a liar, so she'll go to prison and everybody will be happy."

'I took a risk: "You don't seem very happy with that."

'He wasn't. "As far as I'm concerned," he said, "liar or not, she's crazy. She's mad or she's playing a crazy game. Which means she is crazy. Or God knows what. This case is ..." He tapped the pen down sharply on his desk. "I'm sick of this case. There aren't any bodies. No Kate, no John. I don't even know if there's a crime. If the prosecution didn't tell me there was a crime, I wouldn't imagine there was one. Can you see one? I'd be happy to accept your client was hunched over a desk at the BNCF when whatever happened here happened. Only there is no proof."

'"There's no proof she was here, either."

'"What can I say? Your colleague says she is a liar. Listen, I've enough on my plate with what's going on in Camaiore. You know, the other business where there are ..." he shook his head, "... bodies." He shrugged: "Another dead, this morning. Another woman. I have the bodies of two dead women and I know they have nothing to do with your client. It would, however, be convenient for the Chief Prosecutor if your client could carry the blame for everything." He paused. "Tell me, Mr Katiwa, please." He tapped down the pen again. "What are you doing here?"

'My mind felt blank.

'He opened the drawer of his desk and took out a packet of Marlboro, offered me one and I refused. He took one for himself. Marlboro were too much for me. I noticed his lighter, a Zippo.

'I told him I agreed with him. I thought Louise was innocent. *I* felt responsible for the report saying she wasn't.

'"But you didn't write it." He reached around, pushed open the little window behind him and breathed out a mouthful of smoke.

'I shook my head. "You're right. I didn't write it, but I work with the man who did."

'"So," he said. "You want to stab him in the back? What's he done to you?"

'I didn't reply.

'"Surely this is ridiculous," he said. "He's written a report and you say you don't agree with it. You weren't even here."

'"I've listened to the tape."

'He drew on his cigarette and breathed out slowly. "I listen to a lot of tapes," he said. "Music in my car. But can I dance? Can I? Fuck." He looked at his watch. "What do you want from me?"

'"Her solicitor wants me to write another report."

'"Your colleague will love you. But fine. The world moves on." He glanced at his watch again. "I've got work to do. These women in Camaiore ... there's a man out there who's very sick. I don't think he is interested in people like Kate or John. I'm sure he's not interested in *men.*" He stressed the word so the letter buzzed in the air on its own, like an insect. "Which is lucky for you. And for me. But not for the women he's killed. You can see Miss Finnegan as often as you like. Maybe they'll be moving her on for trial soon. I don't know. I am just a policeman, and this is Italy. Here." He scribbled his signature on a form and handed it to me. "You talk to her as often as you like.""'

*

I was suddenly conscious of Kay. While I was speaking she hadn't said a word. I looked at her.

She smiled. 'I'm imagining it. What did you do next?'

'I went back to my hotel on the other side of Pisa.'

'No.'

I looked across at her. Her eyes were closed. 'Tell me properly,' she said. 'In detail.'

In detail?

'Please.'

'I walked back into the courtyard.' The scene was there like a film.

'I looked at the police cars, then up at the wall of the villa. There on the second floor was the window of the room where I'd talked to Louise. Above it was the room where she was kept.

'I put my hands into my pockets and stood in the shade having a cigarette. I looked around me. There were a couple of officers talking to each other in one corner of the courtyard, one in a sentry box at the gate, wide open, leading out onto the main road. Nobody was interested in me. I focused my eyes on the cobblestones, and let my gaze go soft, and I listened.

'There were cars, there were men talking – the officers at the gate I assumed. I heard someone typing in the building behind me, maybe Semproni, but I didn't let that thought go any further. All I wanted to do, actually ...'

Kay touched my leg. 'What did you want to do?'

'I don't know.'

'What did you do?'

'I listened. The officers were still talking.' It all came back to me as clearly as if I was there. 'There was a tap running somewhere. There was a drill, some builders. There was a door closing. And there was a jet high above me, rumbling, which I thought was thunder.

'I thought about me in the universe ... and the universe in me. I remembered my old psychotherapist. She said: *You're the sun*? I say yes. *So, where's your father then*? I tell her: Mars. *No*, she says. *You don't think like that.*

'No. I don't. If Dad was anywhere, he was everywhere, like Dark Matter. He was invisible. A lot heavier than you could imagine.'

I was sick of talking. I wanted Kay to read my mind.

Then something took me back into the present: someone ripping a sheet of paper, maybe the typist, unhappy with what they'd typed – a bad report like Simon's. I caught the sound of another airplane, this one not a jet but one with propellers, like a tractor. A dog barked a long way off, outside the courtyard, almost an echo of itself.

What was I feeling? It was an old feeling. You've started something ridiculous and everybody's going to have a good laugh. You clown.

I was conscious of the cobblestones again and a pair of shining black shoes. I glanced up. It was the officer from the sentry box.

He said something in Italian.

I told him I was sorry, that I was just thinking.

He replied in English, scrutinising me: 'You OK?'

I told him I was fine.

'You look tired.'

'Maybe I am.'

'You know,' he said, turning away, 'you waste your time.' He kept talking as he walked back towards his post. 'If I you, I get myself some sleep. The woman, she's guilty. Or maybe,' he continued almost to himself, 'you have fallen in love?' He laughed.

So I went back to my hotel. I walked through the old town, with its arcaded streets, and kept going toward the cathedral. It was hot. I felt the sweat running down my back, but walking seemed good. I was only feeling half the loser I had been at the police station. The further I got, the more columns there were between me and Louise, the less stupid I felt. I was heading towards the tower.

Since I'd arrived in Pisa I'd probably seen as many pictures of the leaning tower as I'd seen pictures of any one thing in my life: postcards, posters, t-shirts, models on tourist stands. Even the taxi I'd taken from my hotel to the police station had a little golden tower dangling from its rear-view mirror.

I walked three or four times around it, watching people having their photographs taken – playing tricks with the perspective: as if they were holding the tower up, or pushing it down. They pretended to push in various places, whoever held the camera directing them like they were making a film. All of those people leaning into space, I thought. I felt like that. I'd committed myself to something; I was there in Pisa. But what was it?

At the hotel I checked in and headed up to my room. It was pleasant enough, but something about it bothered me. The corridor from the lift to my room seemed too narrow.

The walls felt too close as I walked down it. Then there was the door to my room. It was too thin: six inches narrower than what I'd call a door.

Doing this for the second time, all the narrowness seemed far more irritating than when I'd first arrived. I was tired then, when I'd checked in, and the tinnyness of the lift, which shook far too easily when I stepped into it, the tightness of the corridor, and the weasel door – these were things that didn't seem to bother me as much as the room itself.

It felt dreadful: far too hot, and I was sweating even more, saturated. The air in my lungs felt too warm. I opened the window so I could look down on the street, and it didn't feel any cooler, but at least the room felt bigger – as long as I didn't look across the street. There was a white wall, the paint on it peeling, no windows.

I sat on my bed and looked around.

The bed took up most of the room. It was soft, but in a way that suggested it might be ready to give out completely. I lay back, and thought about things – my eyes travelling over the furniture: the little desk with its worn baize surface and what would, anywhere else, have been a perfectly respectable chair. In there, though, it felt too large.

There was a wardrobe, again far too big for the room, and there was my bag, sitting in front of it – the black leather holdall I always carried around with me, even when I wasn't travelling. Italian, soft leather. Sometimes I liked to put it down and use it as a pillow, turning my head so I felt the cool material on my skin.

In it were the things I always travelled with: my notebook, a Sony Walkman and headphones, my little tape recorder, my toiletry bag, and my aftershave. At that time I wore something French called Bandit that I liked very much. It sort of rhymed with laundry. I don't think, even then, I could have worn it pronounced the English way.

I had the tapes, too.

I sat up and reached over for my bag, opened it and took out the tapes and my Walkman, and the headphones. I always kept them unplugged, the wire carefully wound up so it wouldn't tangle. Then I pushed everything to one side, went to the window and leaned out to get some fresh air. Why did I feel trapped?

Perhaps I should ask for a larger room.

I noticed the tapes again. Then the Walkman. I sat down, plugged in the headphones and placed them over my ears. The grey sponge felt sticky. I picked up the tape Simon had made: *Louise: Pisa.*

I knew what I wanted to listen to: Louise describing how John disappeared. I'd already listened to that section maybe two dozen times, so it didn't take long for me to find the right place on the tape, just about. I pressed play and I heard Louise speaking – it wasn't quite the right place.

Where was I?

I'd felt as if I was back in Pisa. I was in bed with Kay, the tape recorder balanced on my stomach.

Kay shifted. 'Can we hear more?' She sounded sleepy.

'You want to.'

'Yes, please.'

'What do you want to listen to?'

'Anything.'

I fumbled for the tape recorder. She took it from me, shifted it to her own belly. Without the weight I felt lighter, dizzy. She loaded the tape.

'Kay?'

'What is it?' she murmured. I heard a click.

I asked where we were.

She told me she was finding the place.

'The place on the tape,' I said.

'Yes, the place on the tape.'

Another click:

LOUISE

They turned so the city seemed to roll and for a moment she felt she might lose all sense of herself, and then she felt nothing at all, like a hazy day by a river, she thought, like lying under a tree looking up at the leaves, a safe feeling of not feeling, as though she was being carried in magic arms ...

The tape stopped.

'*Where* are we?'

'Here.'

She presses the forward button, then lets go. Click. Play:

LOUISE

... the sound of the birds, the dawn chorus, had been overwhelming. More like a rhythm than a tune ...

It stopped again.

'What are you looking for?'

'I don't know.'

The sound of the birds was ringing in my ears. Now it's silent.

I'm staring through the window into the sunlight, at the sky, remembering what John said: 'Listen to that. Listen to the birds.' When did he say that? He isn't here. I remember he got out of bed.

Click. Play.

LOUISE

It had almost been dark. It had been dawn, just before dawn, that Kate had seen him, there, in front of the window.

The whole memory began to return. Something had drawn her attention: a shape above John's bare shoulder. She raised herself up on and stared down the bed towards where he'd been standing. It almost came as a surprise for him not to be there – but there was the shape, the rectangle. The dark frame of a painting which she hadn't noticed when they arrived, in that whirl of the moment, tearing off each other's clothes. A woman wearing a necklace with what looked like a little gold book hanging from it.

She sat up properly. It was easy to see how she missed the painting when they arrived. They'd been exhausted and it was all undressing, touching, almost in a trance and not really taking anything in. She hadn't liked it at all. It hadn't felt like them, the way they usually made love. He'd felt distant, only it wasn't really about distance. It was as if something was going on that was too much for them. She had felt so tired.

The days before at Wasing felt as if she'd invented them, as though there was nothing to them. She thought of her wedding dress. Why did that make her think of her wedding dress? She thought about the silk of her wedding dress and burst into tears.

The dress was in a black bag.

SIMON

The wedding dress?

LOUISE

After the wedding we had drinks at Wasing. It was a small party, just a few friends, and then Kate and John changed and got a taxi to the airport. She asked if I'd look after the dress, and I said I would, and she picked this black bin bag off the floor. I hadn't even noticed it. She'd been saying goodbye with it down by her feet near the wall, as though it had rubbish in it. She held it up for me, the neck all twisted round, and the dress screwed up inside. The zip was broken.

SIMON
You checked?

LOUISE
Yes, of course I did. When I went back to Wasing I hung it up. It was torn. It doesn't matter. I went to Wasing, then I got my own flight.

SIMON
To Italy as well?

LOUISE
Yes, I went to Pisa, too. Then to Florence by train.

SIMON
Where you were working?

LOUISE
I was at the BNCF. I went there after the wedding – nothing to do with them.

SIMON
The BNCF?

LOUISE
The *Biblioteca Nazionale Centrale di Firenze.* It's one of the main libraries in Europe. I was researching something about the Medicis.

SIMON
I see.

LOUISE
So I was in Italy. But it's got nothing to do with this.

SIMON
The police can't find any record of you being in the library.

LOUISE
I was there. I was at a hotel there.

SIMON
Yes, they agree. But that doesn't prove anything.

[Silence]

LOUISE
I need to tell you what happened to Kate.

[Silence, interminable.]

SIMON
Louise?

LOUISE
Huh?

SIMON
What about Kate?

LOUISE *[Hesitant.]*
I can only tell you what she told me.

SIMON
OK.

LOUISE
She was in bed in the Villa Inghilterra. A bit chilly. And –

I don't know where John is. I'm not in the Langham. I sit up – I'm shivering, like a kind of a leaf, holding on to his letter – the lovely note he wrote me. I woke up and he was gone but there was the letter, on his pillow. I look around the room from my bed-tree and think how strange it seems, being in Italy at last. I'm in the villa and I'm alone, in bed, wrapped up in a sheet. A leaf. It's quiet.

Where is he? I'm tight: tight in myself like I'm corkscrewed, one leg wound around the other.

I hear footsteps. He's coming. They're his: soft and muffled as if he has cotton feet. He walks in a way where he puts down one foot more heavily than the other, but he doesn't stomp. I see the door handle turning and I imagine myself sitting here; and I'm sitting up now holding onto his letter – yes he is here. He smiles – nervously; he walks over to our bags and crouches, rummaging in one of them.

'John?' I sound anxious.

'Sorry.' The smile leaves him for a moment, then it comes back. I'm loosening, softening.

'Where've you been?'

'I had to go outside. It's so beautiful here.'

Why doesn't he mention the note he left behind? 'I found it,' I say, holding it out. 'You found my letters.' He's written a reply to my last letter. The last of my letters to his father.

'Your letters,' he says. 'I found them at Wasing.' Why does he sound guilty? Oh – and what's that? I can hear Louise.

LOUISE
At the wedding reception John told me how he'd found Kate's notebook. Two nights before the wedding he couldn't sleep and had got up in the middle of the night, sat on that little Lloyd Loom chair in their bedroom, and found her notebook lying open there. *[Pause.]* She must have forgotten about it. *[Pause.]* He couldn't help looking at it and seeing what was written there, in the moonlight; and at first it didn't make sense. What was he reading? They read like love letters. He read from the beginning, glancing over to Kate, checking she was still asleep. The first page had several sentences written on it. None of them seemed related, some, false starts, were crossed out. Kate moved, so he picked up the book and went down to the library where he read on.

One sentence on the first page stood on its own, underlined: *Sonnets from the Portuguese.* And then in French: *Les Lettres Portugaises.* Both seemed to be written with very little conviction, a bit of a scrawl.

That was when he came to see me.

SIMON
He came to see you?

LOUISE
I was there, remember? He woke me up, knocking. I was in one of the rooms at the back of the house, well out of

earshot of their room. He was knocking frantically, as loud as he could. I told him to come in; he was in a state. He had the book in his hand and he threw it down on my bed before I could even turn the light on.

'What's this?' he demanded. I hadn't seen him like that before, angry as hell. He frightened me.

I knew what it was straight away. I told him. I explained what the Sonnets from the Portuguese are and why she might have written that on the first page. It's the Brownings, I told him. *[Pause.]* Do you know what they are?

SIMON
No, I don't.

[Simon sounds irritated. Never much of a reader.]

LOUISE
Kate loved Browning almost as much as Peter Fraser. The Sonnets were a series of poems Elizabeth Barrett Browning wrote for Robert Browning before they were married – and then presented them to him as a wedding gift. I explained to John that Kate was doing very nearly the same thing, for him: writing love letters to him as if he'd been writing to her.

SIMON
Did he believe you?

LOUISE
Not at first. Of course not. I had to take him back to the library and show him a copy of the Browning. Then he believed me, we had a cup of tea, and everybody went back to bed.

SIMON
Kate didn't know about this?

LOUISE
John didn't want to spoil the surprise. He put the notebook back where he found it, went back to bed, and that was that.

SIMON
Why didn't you just tell her the truth? Kate was writing an academic project responding to the letters of a dead poet.

LOUISE
Because if I'd done that he might have twigged that they really were love letters.

[More silence.]

SIMON
Why would she write that at the front of the book? *Sonnets from the Portuguese*?

LOUISE
They were love letters to Jack France.

[Silence.]

SIMON
Did you tell her John knew?

LOUISE
I didn't get a chance.

SIMON
You didn't get a chance?

LOUISE
No I didn't.

John's here, now, looking at me – and I have his note in my hand.

'I was going to show them to you,' I say. 'All of them.'

'I know.' He sounds flustered, as though he'd rather not be speaking about them. 'It's all right,' he says. 'I know what the *Sonnets from the Portuguese* are.'

He understands.

After all, Louise told him. Did she? How did she? I heard her say so ...

I want to jump to my feet. I want to kiss him. 'They're lovely,' I say. 'They're perfect. And what you've done for me – what you've done for me ...' I hold up the sheet of paper and put it on the pillow beside me. 'It's perfect.'

He looks puzzled. He looks worried, as though he doesn't get it. What's there to get?

He breaks the silence: 'I think we should go into town.'

I hold on; I want something else to happen. Perhaps it will. Something magical: petals, sparkles. When it still hasn't I fold up the sheet of paper carefully and hold onto it, as though it's a little bird. 'It's beautiful.'

He nods slowly.

'You look like I'm going to tell you off,' I say.

'Do I?' He laughs. 'I'm relieved you don't mind. I shouldn't have read any of it.'

Now I feel confused. What is that I don't understand? I wonder: are those your thoughts? He watches me, trying to read me. What's he looking for?

Does it matter? It's as if the letters have done something all of their own.

*

I was next to Kay. Where?
  'Next to *me*.'
In the Langham. She was forwarding the tape, as if she knew where to head for. Stop, pause. She's sobbing.
  'Kay?
  'No, it doesn't matter. You need to listen.'
  'But you're crying. You were crying back in Harley Street.'
  'I'm remembering, too.'
  Click. Play:

LOUISE *[Hesitant, gentle.]*
They were by the pool the next day.

[I listen and I'm with her words again I'm ...]

I'm lying on my back by the pool, staring through a threadbare parasol. Here and there, there are holes, so I can see the sky – and the spokes are showing all along the edges.
  Who else has lain like this? Over the years people bathing, people lying like me, together or on their own. I'm on the sun terrace – I love the sound of that: Sun Terrace. And something distracts me: an eagle flying high above me. A great bird gliding on the air currents over the Villa Inghilterra.
  'Kate?'
  I look round. John levers himself onto his elbows. We're the only people beside the pool.

I was thinking about his note that I found this morning. His lovely note. I'd been thinking about his father's letters. About K. And then I was staring up through the parasol.

He asks me: 'How cold do you think the water is?' He's wearing sunglasses. He's smiling; I wish I could see his eyes. He stares at the pool; the water's so blue.

I can see right down to the bottom.

I swing my feet onto the grass and feel how warm it is – as if I'm touching somebody. I stand. I feel rather dizzy. John sees this:

'Are you all right?'

'I'm fine.'

Before we came down to the pool I wasn't feeling too good. We went into town so he could see Christina, and he got lost. I needed to rest so we came back and lay by the pool, here.

I want to swim and I go to the edge, put my hands on my hips, and stand very still. The surface ripples. I make a shape with my fingers.

'What's that?'

'A happy shape.' I dive, and I hit the water, and I make a star, and I'm going down. My eyes are closed and I'm sinking; I let myself go. I feel the air emptying out of my lungs, bubbles trailing from my nose. The noise is so strange, as if everything has slowed down, like a tape recorder winding down. Are those the bubbles or are they voices? I don't know as I slowly slip away.

My toes touch the tiles and I open my lips; and I feel the water in my mouth – I want to shout and I kick: I kick and shoot to the surface, and gasp, shaking my head, my hair whipping the water. I spit. I look where I think John is but he isn't there: it's somebody else. I scream and dive backwards, thrashing. It's Jack: I can see Jack France.

'Jack!'

'Kate!'

It's John.

He stares at me. 'What is it?'

'Something scared me.' My arms, my legs are stiff. Suddenly I'm cold. I'm gripping the edge of the pool as if I'm about to be dragged away.

'What is it?' He looks unsure, as though he's trying to read me, like he did back in the bedroom after I found the note.

'I didn't know it was you.'

'Me?'

'You didn't look like you.' I'm starting to relax; I let go of the gutter and bob, my shoulders dipping under the surface; the dripping of water around my ears. I rest my head back so it floats and I tread water. 'Come in,' I ask him.

He hesitates, steps forward and drops into the water. He's beside me. I reach out and touch the side of his face. It's wet as if he's been crying; although I know it's water from the pool. He touches my face. We're both treading water. I can feel the sun on us and it's so beautiful here, the water lapping at the edges and far away I can hear birds in the trees; the sound of a car: a motor put-putting through the woods at the bottom of the valley.

We swim and play for a while then John goes back to the Villa. I listen to him climb steps, the flat noise of his sandals sounding tired. I roll onto my side and stare at the pool. It looks fiery. I'm waiting for something to happen. I know because I remember it coming to me at the bottom of the pool; not so I can think about it – not like that. Not so I can really remember it. But it was there. Like a rose; like a flower I couldn't pick. And as I lie there it's as if something is swelling in me, waiting to happen. It's going to happen.

I saw Jack. It was him. I can feel my heart. My heart's like a little bird drumming its wings: Hummingbird. I remember seeing Jack and I find myself looking down at me in the water. I'm looking out of his eyes.

Whose eyes?

I reach into my bag and take out my notepad. I unclip my pen from the cover, turn to a clean page and start to write: I saw you, you know. I saw you above me and you saw me.

I stop – the tip of my pen hovering over the page. The *you* I am writing to is different from the one I wrote to in England. In England I have been writing to Jack. Now: who am I writing to? John.

I write so quickly it's as if I'm taking notes, my mind a moment ahead of the words appearing on the page in front of me, a fraction of a moment, so small it makes no difference.

I drop my pen. My fingers ache: two pages, a compulsion. My forehead feels damp, sweaty, as if I am ill, and I close my eyes. The light feels too bright – too bright to bear. I get to my feet, stride to the edge of the pool, step from the edge and plunge into the water. The cold shock of it makes me gasp and I close my eyes. There's no one to hear or watch me so I let myself sink again, down to the bottom, slowly, so the air drains from my body, my arms and legs like string. My breasts touch the bottom, then my toes, and finally my face – and the water feels dangerous.

If I draw breath I'll be dead. If I don't rise up soon that's what will happen, but I don't feel frightened. There is a breath which I can take, which a drowning person can take. When they do, their lungs fill up.

I let myself rise and I break the surface. I take a long, slow breath shielding my eyes because the sun seems to be brighter still. And there's John at the top of the stairs walking along the path leading to the terrace. I wave to him but he's facing away from me, towards the tower. I try to call out but the sun's in my eyes, I lose my balance, I swallow a mouthful of water and slip back under the surface. When I rise again, coughing, he's gone. I look around; maybe he's gone back inside. So I swim to the side, climb out and dry myself.

In a hurry I pack my things, wrap myself in my blue sarong and make my way up the steps towards the hotel. By the time I reach the top I'm breathless; and there's the woman who owns the hotel, watering some plants.

I ask her if she's seen John: he must've walked past. The watering can's dripping small dark shapes onto the ground. They disappear.

'He left the hotel a few minutes ago.'

'Did he say where he was going?'

She sees the water spattering on the floor and tilts the nozzle of her watering can up. One last droplet falls; we both notice it at the same time.

'He didn't. He didn't notice me.'

'Oh.'

I touch the back of my neck and feel dizzy.

'Are you burning?'

I'm not sure if I hear the question right; I seem to be missing something.

She touches my forehead. 'Are you okay?'

I start to massage my neck. I press my thumb against my cheek and open my mouth to say something – but nothing comes out. I'm squinting. The light's too sharp.

'I think, maybe, you've been out in the sun too long. Come inside, have a seat in the lounge where it's cool. I'll see if I can find your husband.'

'He was here.'

'Where?'

'Yes. I'm sure, he was here.' I don't sound convincing – even to me. I stare at the tarpaulin around the top of the clocktower. 'Is it broken?'

The woman takes hold of my wrist and draws me forward. She glances up at the top of the tower. I take a couple of steps and I'm right next to the scaffolding. I ask her: 'Why are there buckets up there?' There are two, one perched at either end of the platform.

She doesn't seem interested in what I'm saying. She tugs and mutters something I can't understand. I'm frightened. I'm really scared: everything is toppling over. The tower is coming down on top of us; there, it's lurching. I stare around us. It's like a film with bits cut out; or maybe there aren't those bits. There's nothing there. My knees go.

There's somebody running towards us. I look: it isn't John. It isn't Jack. It's nobody.

*

The tape stopped. Kay was touching her necklace.

'Who are you?' I asked.

'I'm Kay.'

'You're Kate?'

'I'm Kay – Kay.' Her fingers moved on the tape recorder; the tape shuttled forwards. She pressed play. 'Here.'

'Where?'

'This is Semproni.'

There's the hiss:

LOUISE

Kate couldn't remember the detective's rank, even though she was sure she'd been told it twice –

– it is. It's the second time he's said so.

He's speaking perfect English; I can't believe it. His voice is very soft but what he's saying is in English. I'm sitting on an armchair, a small coffee table between me and the detective and the man sitting beside him. Behind them are books – a whole wall, a little library. The detective's got a black beard. It's not thick, exactly, but it's heavy. He takes a long breath and smiles, gently.

'Mrs France, before we go any further there are some things I need to ask you.'

His assistant is reading something. It's John's passport.

I can't stop myself: 'Where did you get that?'

The assistant, a stocky man, his shirt a little too small for him, looks at the detective – who answers for him.

'I asked for it. They gave it to me at reception. We'll need a photograph, unless you have another?' He takes the passport and hands it to me. 'You want to hold onto it?'

I thank him, take it and set it on my lap. 'What do you want to know?'

'I'm sure you're anxious. We'll do all we can to work this out as quickly as we can.' He nods, professionally. 'When was the last time you saw your husband?'

'I was in the pool. I saw him looking at the tower.' I raise my hand towards the window; it's dark but we can see the edge of the tower. 'Would you like me to show you?'

'Later, perhaps.' He tilts his head slightly to one side. 'You're here on your honeymoon, right?'

'That's right.'

'And you've been here for one day?'

'Yes this was our first day.'

'I see.'

His colleague says something in Italian that I can't catch. I hardly know any Italian. The detective waits a moment, as if to let what his colleague has said sink in. Then he speaks. 'Before I ask you anything else, and I can imagine how terrible this is for you, let me please explain something.'

I nod.

'Some serious crimes have been committed. When something like this happens all kinds of people are drawn to a place. These disappearances. People can't help themselves. Some of them want to help. Some of them want to take responsibility. They walk into the police station and say, to a man such as my assistant here: it's me. I did it. In most cases we simply ask the person involved to take a seat, in a cell if that makes them happiest.

'So your husband – your husband has disappeared. If you honestly believe your husband is missing, that something has happened to him, that is one thing. But if, for example, there is a problem between you, or he has any kind of a problem which would mean he might prefer to be lost, on his own, then please tell me.'

'No. There's nothing.' I feel so completely cold. I can barely hear him. He feels hundreds of miles away.

'I'm sorry to have to say these things. Occasionally, and I can think of a number of cases, people come to the place like this, at a time like this, specifically to disappear. It's very sad, but they do. One tragedy,' he shrugs, 'can attract another. They come together like a family.' He closes his eyes and then he looks straight at me. 'Most of the time, things are anything but straightforward.'

'My husband has disappeared.' I'm hot now, angry; my voice shakes. 'He's been gone for at least six hours and I can think of no reason – absolutely no reason at all – why he isn't here. He didn't say he was going. We were by the pool and he went back to the hotel to get something.'

'He didn't leave a note?'

The note. 'No. Not when he went.'

The detective tilts his head again. 'Not when he went?'

'No.'

'But?'

I feel John's passport bend as I squeeze it.

'Please be careful with that.' He nods towards the passport. 'We may need it.'

I let it rest on my legs and stare out of the window, looking for something to help me.

'Did he leave a note, Mrs French?'

'I said no, not when he left. He gave me something this morning. He left a note on the pillow in our bed.'

'Oh? Do you have it?'

'It's upstairs in my room.'

'Can I see it?'

'It isn't about any of this.'

'Even so, I'd better take a look. My assistant will fetch it if you tell him where it is.'

'I'd rather get it myself.'

'No.' The detective cuts in as I try to stand up. 'I would rather that you stayed here with me. We can talk about this a little more while he gets it. Please, sit down.'

I lower myself back into my chair.

'Now. Where can we find this note? This letter.'

I tell him about my bag on my bed. 'My notebook's inside. The letter's tucked into a pocket at the back.' The detective slaps his hand down on his assistant, grinning at him. 'I think you should bring us this bag.' He looks back at me. 'I don't want to cause you any more trouble than I have to.'

'Thank you.'

The assistant leaves the room and I'm left facing the detective.

He doesn't miss a beat. 'You're a writer?'

He worries me. 'No. What makes you think that?'

'You've got a notebook. I meet a lot of English men and women with notebooks in Tuscany; most of them tell me they are writers.'

'I'm an academic.'

He nods slowly. 'I've been calling you Mrs France. Should I have said: Dr France?'

Something in me shifts. 'If you like.' I look at him slightly differently, as if he's leaned back a little – as if he's given me more space. 'I don't especially like that kind of thing.'

'The title?'

'Dr – no. I don't like it.'

'But it's something special, isn't it?'

I don't reply straight away. I'm looking into his eyes, wondering what's going on. I want John. Why is he talking to me like this? I say, 'I suppose so.'

'I studied at Oxford,' he says.

'So did I.'

'A coincidence.'

It feels uncomfortable. I'm not sitting properly – not how I like it. His assistant left the door open and outside I can hear creaks and footsteps, the sounds of people moving awkwardly, going from room to room. I imagine everybody around the hotel wondering what's going on – all of the other guests.

Where's John?

I look at the detective as if I'm a child: I know that. I feel so small and young. The armchair feels so large.

The assistant walks back into the room holding my bag in both hands as if he is scared he might drop it. The detective smiles and nods at me. 'Maybe you can find the letter for us?'

I still have John's passport on my knee.

'Here.' The detective leans across. 'Let me take that –' he takes the passport, brushing my leg with his fingertips. I don't know if he meant to. I can't tell from his eyes – his expression. He doesn't look interested in me like that. He watches the assistant hand me my bag. I take out my notebook and open it at the back page where the letter was tucked away.

It's not there.

He can tell as soon as I realise – I wonder what I look like.

'What is it?' He looks irritated and waves for his assistant to close the door. His voice is a little louder.

'It isn't here.'

'No?' The detective closes his hands around the passport. 'Where else might it be?'

'I don't know.' I leaf through the notebook quickly, fumbling while they watch.

'You write a lot,' he says.

I'm reading something on every page, not sure why I am but reading – maybe it's all I can do. I look at him. I blush. 'It's my work.' I put my notebook down on the table.

'Of course.' The notebook's still open. He reaches out and shifts it towards him. 'These things you have written, I can't help noticing; they also look like letters to me.'

'Yes. Please,' I try to take the notebook back but he picks it up and sits it on his lap, on top of the passport. 'May I have it back please?'

'In a moment.' He turns the pages. 'These look like love letters.' He reads the first page. 'What have you written here: *Sonnets from the Portuguese*?'

I stick my hand in my bag. 'This is all private.'

He ignores me, flicking through the pages. '*Sonnets from the Portuguese*?'

'They're poems.' I dump my bag on the floor with a thud.

'Here,' he says, as if I haven't said anything. '*The Sonnets from the Portuguese*. Here, on the first page, where a title would be.'

'*The Sonnets from the Portuguese* are poems.'

'I know,' he says. 'Sonnets, I would have thought ...' he hands the notebook back to me '... are always poems.'

I blush and put the notebook back in my bag.

'No sign of a letter from your husband though.'

'No.'

'Perhaps you can remember what he said to you? In his letter.' The assistant sits back down next to the detective, takes out his notebook and holds a stubby black biro poised on the page.

'It was a love letter.'

'A love letter? You must be very sorry to have lost it.'

I turn away. There's a little mirror on the wall furthest from me, reflecting the light from a lamp. I stare at it and speak slowly. 'John knows how important writing is to me – so he wrote to me. This is our honeymoon.'

'I see. But what did the letter say?'

I'm not going to tell him what John said to me. I lie: 'He said he had read the letters I was writing. The ones in my notebook. These ones.' I put my hand inside my bag and touch the notebook. 'And he said that they're beautiful.'

'So those letters, the ones in your notebook, are for him, your husband? Like the *Sonnets from the Portuguese* were love letters to Mr Browning?'

I don't know what to say. He'd seen what I had written: *Sonnets from the Portuguese*. My project feels strange, dirty.

'Who are the letters to?' He looks curious. 'Your husband seems to believe that they were for him – and I would think that's reasonable, if I found the notebook and saw what you've written at the front. *Sonnets from the Portuguese*; and in French: *Les Lettres Portugaises*. I assume your husband is the kind of man who knows these things?'

I answer too quickly: 'Of course he does.'

'Or even if you look them up. Maybe this is the kind of thing you talk about, as an academic? I would imagine you discuss it more, perhaps, than who has topped the pop charts.' He stands up and looks out of the window. 'I love thee to the depth and breadth and height my soul can reach.' He pauses and then looks back at me. 'That's right, isn't it?'

I nod, surprised.

'I believe the idea came from some love letters reputed to have been written by a Portuguese nun. And the Brownings came here, to Tuscany, like a lot of you English do. She was a bit of a nun, wasn't she?' He walks towards the door. 'I'm going to look for your husband.' He checks his watch. 'I think he would have been back by now if he could.' He glances at his assistant. 'Perhaps you could ask Dr France precisely what her husband was doing when she last saw him. And what he was wearing. He bows his head and leaves.

I look at the assistant. 'He is horrible.'

'My boss?'

'Of course I mean your boss.'

'He's not so bad. Now, please, tell me when you last saw your husband.'

*

153

I felt breath on my shoulder. Kay was sleeping. She held her necklace, her eyelids flickering. Ghosts dream. I felt so tired –

– and I'm watching something; something happening in the dark, somebody sweeping a torch over the surface of the swimming pool at the hotel. Semproni, the detective. I remember his name. I watch him wave his torch and then I go back inside, from my balcony.

I lock the door and quietly, carefully, I start to pull the room to pieces.

I take a pillow from the bed, pull off its case, shake it and fetch a nail file from my toilet bag. I slash away so the cotton lies like bandages on the bedroom floor. I want to see inside the pillow. I'm looking for the letter. There is nothing in the pillow. So I pick up the other one and cut it – just once and plunge my hand inside it, into the feathers. There's nothing there and I throw it against the wall so it explodes. Feathers fill the air. I pick it up and go to the door. I can't bear to have the thing in there with me. I unlock the door, throw it open and toss both of the pillows out. I drag the duvet from its cover and tear it to pieces, too. The strips look remarkable on the floor, like flower petals. I take the sheet from the bed and fling it over my shoulder; it catches on the wardrobe. I lift the mattress off the bedstead and prop it against the chest of drawers.

I can see through the bed. There's nothing underneath it apart from a pair of John's black Chelsea boots. I sit on the mesh covering the springs, hugging my knees to my chest and listening to the bed creak as I rock.

*

How long have I been doing that? I don't know. I get up, awkwardly. I fall off the bed. I take the top drawer of the little cabinet on my side of the bed and throw its contents into the bath. And, as if I'm stirring something, I run my hands through all the things in there: a Bible, some paper, a pencil, a postcard and some junk from my pockets. Coins and a bottle opener and some leaflets from Camaiore. I go back to the cabinet and open the compartment below. There's nothing there. I heave the mattress back across the bed and rest it against the door.

Somebody knocks on the door: 'Would you like a cup of tea?'

'No I don't want a cup of tea.' My voice sounds ordinary.

Whoever it is goes. Then they come back. Then they go.

Now I've moved the mattress, I can get into the chest of drawers. There are four drawers, two of which are empty. The two that are full – I empty them into the bath. They contain some clothes, mainly underwear. Neither of us have unpacked properly. Not yet, we haven't. So I go to our bags and tip those onto the bedstead, throwing off one thing after another once I've checked the pockets, the sleeves, and every fold to make sure nothing is there.

I see John's brick of a phone. He doesn't have it with him. I pick it up and sit at the end of the bed staring into the mirror and tipping everything that's in my handbag out onto my lap. All of the things fall between my thighs. I pick up the phone and throw it against the wall. It smashes. Its pieces fall amongst the strips of bed sheet and the feathers – fragments of plastic everywhere and there's a mark like a bruise on the wall.

I pick up what's left of the phone, study it, and wonder if I can still use it. I'll ring Louise:

'Hello?'

She sounds happy. She says she's in Florence, working at the library. Then, when I don't say anything, she sounds different. I don't say much; I tell her I really need her. I say that John's disappeared. She doesn't understand. I say again. 'John's disappeared.' She tells me she's coming. She's coming from Florence; she's been in Florence, at the library, since we were in Wasing.

I start to cry.

*

How long have I been crying? I don't know. Somebody taps at the door again.

'Is everything all right?' It's a woman.

I sound calm, I think. 'Everything's fine.'

'We wondered if you'd like to come downstairs.'

'No thank you.'

She goes. I listen to her footsteps growing distant. I lie back on the bedstead.

Have I been sleeping?

Somebody's here.

I want to sit up – I can't. My eyes are open. I can't close them. I'm looking at the ceiling; at a particular spot on the ceiling: a circle of light, as if somebody is shining a torch there, sometimes losing their concentration and it moves. And they correct it.

I can't speak.

My lips are stuck together and my tongue's cold. I can hear myself breathing.

It isn't my breathing. There is somebody else here; I can't breathe. There's somebody else here, like at Wasing.

It sounds like a machine.

No answer. The light on the ceiling shivers and wobbles.

It's gone dark.

It's so silent. I'm lying here ... and I'm lying here and they kicked the door down.

'He was here,' I say.

It's the detective. 'Your husband was here?'

I don't reply. I don't know what to say.

*

Where's Kay? I'm lying just as I was, but the tape recorder is on my chest; I ease it off as though it has fallen on me. I look up and I see leaf shapes in the plaster around the ceiling. I remember Kay's words as I fell asleep: *it's like we're lying under the tree.* She sounded gentle.

She's gone. And I'm here.

This isn't remembering. I try to sit up – I try to; I can't. I can't move. I try to call out but I can't make a sound.

I'm not on my own.

I can hear breathing. There's somebody sitting at the end of the bed. I feel terrified but absolutely safe; and I know who makes me feel like this: Dad. I think his name: Dad. I can't say it.

My father is sitting at the end of the bed. He doesn't say anything. Then he says my name:

'Chris.'

I can't answer.

'Chris.'

I think: 'What are you doing here?' Either he doesn't hear me or he doesn't want to say anything – but there he is, as much of him as ever, like an animal.

Perhaps it was a dream. Why do I even mention it? Because I will never know. He was gone. And I slept.

CHAPTER 14
PISA, 1986 / LANGHAM, 2010

It's the next day, and I'm standing in front of the mirror in my hotel room – and someone else is here. I'm standing perfectly still, but the room doesn't seem still. I'm ... where? I'm in the room with the awful chair – not the one with the leaves. It's me. I can see myself in the mirror; I can see me: Chris, but I'm a young man again. My stomach's gone flat and my hair's black. I don't look even thirty and, Christ, I look lonely. I sit down hard on the bed.

The curtain shifts. Something feels very strange ... I think: I went to see Louise, yesterday.

But I didn't. I was in Harley Street.

There's a draught, like someone blowing on my cheek. I'm naked. I can feel the air on my back – but my back's to the door not the window. I check my watch.

It's stopped.

You did, you went to see Louise yesterday.

Somebody's talking to me.

You went to see Louise.

There's a voice: older than me – but me. I know me. It's coming from somewhere – I take a look behind me, and up a bit ... somewhere behind my right ear, as if there's a bird on my shoulder and it's taken a step backwards. I'm thinking of a big black parrot.

That's my nose: I have a hooked nose.

I have a hooked nose.

We do.

I'm going mad.

Touch your face.

I touch my face.

Touch other things.

I get up and walk around the room, running my fingers over the bumps along the edge of the mirror, staring at myself and then turning around, pressing down on the bed, pushing my fingers into the blankets.

You're not mad. I can understand why you'd think that, though.

The voice sounds ordinary. I look in the mirror again; and touch the glass. How strange is that? More ordinary than seeing myself as a young man. More ordinary than being in two places at once and, now –

I'm in Pisa. It's hot. The sun's up. People are walking past and yesterday? That seems to be disappearing – and these people, what are they? Ghosts? Their footsteps – imagine; imagine, I once thought, if there was some way of catching up with sound from the past. And you can, in space, apparently. In space, right now, if you had a good enough ear you'd be able to hear the dinosaurs.

And yesterday you saw Louise.

I was with Kay, in Harley Street.

And you were with Kay.

I can't have done both.

I'm thinking, not speaking.

You slept with Kay. You spoke to Louise's solicitor in Semproni's office, went to the interview room, turned your tape recorder on and waited. Louise came in wearing a t-shirt and jeans, her hair tied in a knot as if she was going to do some cleaning. She had a little make-up on but barely enough to hide how tired she felt. And as you thought that, she seemed to get in touch with what you were thinking.

'I've been having nightmares,' she said, folding her arms.

You told her you were sorry to hear that.

She took a breath and crossed her legs. 'It's pretty nasty here.' She looked around the room. 'It could be a lot worse ...' Her voice trailed off. 'But it's pretty nasty.'

You told her you'd listened to the tapes of her speaking to Simon again.

'When?' she asked.

You said the previous night.

She told you that was funny, because that was what she'd dreamed you were doing: listening to her talking to Simon. She asked if you minded being in her dream.

You didn't say anything.

She asked what you'd heard.

You told her you knew about the confusion over the letters. John disappearing. Then you asked her how she knew these things. She hadn't been there.

'Kate told me,' she said. Then she was silent, just long enough for you to start feeling uncomfortable – until she asked: 'Can you help me?'

That got your attention. You said that you thought you could.

'Am I crazy?' she asked. She nodded as though she was talking to herself.

You didn't say anything at first.

'If I'm mad,' she said, 'would you know?'

You told her you could understand how she might feel mad, caught up in something like this.

She asked if her solicitor thought she was mad. You remembered the look on his face when he'd finished speaking. A funny-looking man with a comb-over, like a football club manager, the kind of man who also ran arcades. He looked blank, hopeless as if he'd been kicked out of the league and someone'd hit the triple jackpot on a Monday.

You asked her straight out: 'Did you kill Kate?'

'No,' she said. She didn't move, she didn't look at you.

'Did you kill John?'

'No.'

'Do you know how they died?'

She looked straight at you. 'Yes,' she said. 'I think I do.' Do you remember how you felt when she said that? How you didn't know what to say? You watched her as though she was holding a gun to her head. Do you think she noticed that? Her lips opened up as if she might say something else, but she didn't make a sound.

The two of you sat there like dummies for five minutes. Eventually you snapped out of it. You said: 'You think you do?'

She closed her eyes. 'That's what I told Simon, but he didn't believe me.' You remember how her eyelids fluttered, as if she was dreaming again. Then she opened her eyes and said it another time: 'Can you help me?'

You asked: 'How can I help you?'

'In the dream I had last night,' she said, 'when you were listening to the tapes, you were hearing them differently.

And it was me speaking on the tapes, only I was talking to you, not to Simon. I was talking to you and what I said sounded different. They were the same words – but it sounded different.' She looked around the room and then down at that cowbell you had to call the guard when you wanted to go. Do you remember thinking not to look there, because, if you did, she might think that you wanted to go? So you didn't and she kept talking, watching you. 'I was saying the same things,' she said, 'because they're true, and I know they're true, but you heard them differently. That's why I'd like you to help me. Because it would be you listening.'

You felt weird: inside you, as if there was something else there, a new moon. You checked the tape recorder and it looked fine, the wheels turning, plenty of tape.

She asked: 'Can I tell it to you now?'

You just nodded.

'It was Jack. Jack France.'

'Jack France?'

'Jack,' she said. 'John's father. He took them. He stole them away from themselves, from each other, from here.' She looked confused. 'You see, it already sounds crazy. How do I sound?'

You told her she sounded different. Like a different person from the one you'd heard on the tapes. Less caught up in something. When you listened to the tapes, you said, it sounded as if she was half-dreaming all the way through.

'That's how it felt,' she said. 'I was frightened. I didn't feel as if I was there. It was like I was floating above myself.'

You told her: 'There was so much detail in everything you said.'

She asked you if being frightened did that.

You said it might.

'I wasn't really aware of what I was saying,' she said. 'I began, and then I talked, and then I got lost ... and then ... I don't know. I stopped. When Simon asked me something, sometimes when he asked me, I didn't know what I'd been saying. I didn't know what he meant. It felt like he was trying to make me say something. Or that he was trying to make something out of what I was saying.'

You felt yourself becoming closer to her. You looked down at her feet. She was wearing sandals, her toenails painted red. You felt a flutter of something, and you ignored it.

'The way you talked,' you said, 'it didn't sound real.'

She put her hand to the side of her face and sighed. Her cheeks tightened. She said she wanted to talk to Semproni again.

You asked what she wanted to tell him.

She said she didn't know, but there had to be something else she could say.

'Like what?' you asked.

She told you she thought Semproni didn't know what Kate was really like, and she told you something about when the two of them were at Oxford.

'The first year we were there she did badly in her Mods,' she said. 'We had a tutor who she'd fallen in with, and she'd been getting very high marks all year. It was a shock for her to do badly, especially when she'd been getting such high marks.'

You asked her if there was something going on between Kate and the tutor.

She said there wasn't.

You asked her if she was sure.

Louise told you she was very sure because she'd been sleeping with him, herself. 'Kate should have got something outstanding,' she said, 'but what she got was just fairly good.'

You asked her what she was trying to say.

She said the tutor deliberately marked Kate down in her exams. He was an expert on Jack France and although it suited him to have someone like Kate thinking about France as beautifully, as clearly, and as imaginatively as she did, it didn't suit him to have anyone else think that. She told you: 'He stole from her. Kate was like that. She let people in and they stole from her.'

You told her you thought Kate had a certain way of knowing things which involved getting inside people who were already close to them.

'Maybe you should talk to Semproni,' you said. A couple of minutes later a guard knocked on the door. Your time was up. No need for the bell.

Shut up.

Sorry?

I've heard enough and I grab my jeans, a t-shirt, my bag, I get dressed and pull on my shoes.

Don't forget the key.

I throw the key into my bag and head out of the room, slam the door and run down the stairs – like in Harley Street; I'm out of there, past reception, into the sun.

No snow.

'No snow,' I say out loud.

Silence. I'm standing in the street waiting for a reply. People are moving around me. I get the odd strange look: who's this guy standing in the middle of the road? Good question. I think it's me.

There's been no answer.

Car horn.

Shit – I jump out of the way; the car's mirror catches my bag and jerks it off my shoulder. It screeches to a stop. Some fat guy gets out of the passenger door, unhooks my bag and throws it back at me. He screams something, gets back in. The car goes.

Where's the voice gone?

I sit down on a bench.

'Are you there?'

No reply.

'Nobody there?'

Doesn't seem like it.

I take a breath and breathe out very slowly, letting the air hiss between my teeth, roll off my tongue, empty out of my lungs like a tyre going down. I need to get calm and work out what's happening.

Am I remembering this? I'm sure I'm not dreaming. No, I'm not dreaming.

I look about: what's that? The railway station. The station: cordoned off, police standing at the entrance. People starting to gather on the pavement. I was going there later. I check I've got my wallet – what else? My Walkman. The tapes: *Louise: Pisa* and *Louise: Pisa, second time*. The one I've been making – and the labels aren't faded. Why would they be faded?

I get up and join the little crowd which has formed. There's a businessman next to me, smoking and glancing at his watch. I look at mine. It's moving again but the wrong time. I change it then ask the businessman in English what's going on. He shakes his head like people do when they barely understand you, and wonders what to say. My Italian's awful. I thank him and start to turn away, but he touches my shoulder and blows a mouthful of smoke into the air.

'Lupo mannaro,' he says. 'Vulfe.'

I shrug.

Something comes to him: 'Werewolf. Wolf-Man.'

'Woman?'

He stares at me as if I am stupid and shakes his head. 'Wolf-Man.'

'Wolf-Man?'

He looks impatient, glances around and points at an old man selling papers at a newspaper stand. 'There,' he says. 'That man ... there ... he know to say.'

I thank him. Something's happening at the station entrance. Two policemen emerge looking grave – one of them stares out at me and nods: Semproni. I nod back. He goes back inside.

I cross the road and wait while the newspaper seller deals with a couple of customers. A squat little man with bushy eyebrows – there's something wolfish about him. He seems conscious of me standing there. As soon as he's free he turns round and smiles.

'*Buon giorno.*'

'I don't speak Italian. Sorry.'

'That's OK, I can talk to you in English. Which English would you like? English English? American English?' He changes his accent to a kind of American, which oddly, in its comedy, sounds as much like the real thing as it could.

'American,' I reply, amused.

'Then American it is.'

'Can you tell me what's going on over there?'

'Oh,' his accent slips. 'That's very bad.' His expression changes; his face seems to harden. He picks up one of the newspapers, turns to one of the inside pages and fingers a column of text. I read *Camaiore* in the heading but can't make any sense of the other words. There's a black and white photograph of a young woman, vacant-looking, sad, set into the text. Her name stands out – it has to be her name. It stands out but I can't think why. It doesn't mean anything to me: Maria Tomaseli.

The newspaper seller interrupts me: tugs me away.

'Camaiore,' he says, looking towards the railway station, 'Over there you can get the train to Camaiore. And this story is about what happens in Camaiore. A woman killed by somebody, yesterday.' He looks at the picture in the newspaper. 'Yesterday, Maria Tomaseli. I say her name. Another not long ago. I don't know her name. Now it looks as if the killer is maybe *here,* in Pisa.' He shakes his head. 'You want a girl at night, you go over there. This morning they find two of them dead, in there, in the station itself. Two girls.' He crosses himself. 'Some people say that's what happens if you are a hooker.' He shakes his head again. 'Somebody said that to me and I knock their bloody head off. Somebody dies and people start saying it was a little bit like their fault, or a lot, huh?' There are tears in his eyes. 'You know what I mean? People want to blame you for getting killed. Two girls.' He puts the newspaper down and takes somebody's money.

'Why do they call him the Wolf-Man?'

'Because somebody say they heard a man howling like a beast, like a wolf. They found the girls when they were looking for whatever it was making a noise like that. In Camaiore they say that's what they heard and here, now, that's what they heard. Around the town when the women died in Camaiore people say they heard the sound like a wolf. So four people are dead.'

Four people, and Kate and John. He taps the newspaper page again.

An old woman turns up and says something in Italian, waving her hands towards the station and nodding knowingly. He starts saying something back harshly, then stops and looks at me again, as if he's forgotten we were having a conversation.

'Do you want a newspaper?'

I reach into my pocket and hand him some change. He offers me the paper neatly folded, as though it has never been opened, and he walks away. I stare for a moment at the back of his head and then head back to the station.

*

I wait impatiently on the pavement outside the station and it starts to rain: warm rain more like the shower I never had. My t-shirt sticks to my skin as the crowd disperses, slipping away to cafés or God knows where, leaving me almost alone – apart from the old woman who bought the newspaper, a couple, tourists who take plastic macs out of their rucksacks and hold hands in the drizzle. A television van arrives and empties out. I wait. The van goes and the rain stops. The police leave – no sign of Semproni.

I get a ticket for Camaiore, find the platform and walk down the train past several empty carriages, glancing into them and feeling I don't want to get on. I need to, but I don't want to. Then I hear English, two young women, chatting and laughing together with slowly, carefully chosen words in the last carriage before the engine. I get in without them noticing me, catch the fact they are talking about Pasolini's *Medea* – they came to Pisa to see the locations he used – and sit down far away enough for me not to intrude but close enough to hear. Are they English? They're speaking deliberately, as if it isn't their first language and part of the fun they're having is to talk it, exquisitely. But they sound English. Odd.

They're students from Rome. They move on to Terence Stamp and *Teorema*: one of them says she wants to sleep with Terence Stamp, one of them doesn't because he's far too old for her.

I tune out, however much I like the sound of their voices. I've never seen *Medea* – but I've seen *Teorema* and its oddness comes back to me. I can see the tops of the women's heads and I remember the scene of a woman floating near the end, rising high over the farm buildings. I feel like that: as if I'm in a film, defying the laws of gravity.

Where's the voice I heard in my hotel room? My voice. The voice isn't there.

My mind must have drifted. Now I'm thinking of the two girls who died at the station. I wonder if they were anything like the women in front of me. Maybe they were the same age. All I can see is the tops of their heads.

I open my newspaper. There's a picture of Louise on the second page – a couple of columns of text about her. What am I doing, coming out here to rescue her?

I wonder if the voice will tell me.

Nothing.

I think about Louise as I look out of the window, through my reflection in fact, at the fields, the mountains, the green trees, until I realise I'm not thinking about her any more. There's somebody else.

And this is a shock as I haven't thought about her, this other person, for years. For a moment I dodge away from her, back to Louise – I try to. I'm thinking about the woman in Camaiore, the one who died yesterday, Maria Tomaseli, instead. I turn to the page in the newspaper with her picture – then I look away, out of the window, onto the endless yellow corn fields.

Maria Tomaszewki.

Why on earth would I want to think about her? Why?

I can't stop myself.

Maria Tomaszewki. Maria *Tomaseli*. Maria *Tomashevskee*. Maria *Tomaselishevskee*.

I look at the newspaper and the 'why' comes to me like a slap in the face. The first time I saw Maria Stein's face was on the front page of the *Dundee Herald* from 1947. The picture was grainy, sickly-looking and crude, photocopied for me by a kind-hearted man at Dundee Library who I'd contacted after my father had his conviction overturned in the High Court.

I close my eyes and I'm back in the front room of the house where I grew up. This is a memory, I know that for sure. My eyes are shut.

There's my mother. How old am I? My mother. I feel a tug. I don't often think of her. She looks dazed, which isn't surprising: she was usually tranquilized. Self-medicating. A lot of nurses do that. She had as many different kinds of pill in our medicine cabinet as there were – what? I don't know. One of the things about how I grew up: it was madhouse, but lacking in variety. Most things, even the flowers in the garden only came in one kind. Daisies. No, there were a couple of wild roses. I remember those, winding around the garden fence. I called them dragons because their thorns were so huge.

Medicines, though, we did well. And sometimes food.

There's Mum on one of the armchairs in the bay window, net curtains behind her like a sort of suburban mist. She's talking to me wearing a shapeless brown cardigan. She's very overweight, squeezed into some blue slacks. Bare feet. She looks kind, but also kind of stoned. At her funeral the priest got her mixed up with someone else and I had to correct her name. When he was talking about her, he described driving through the little village where she was living and often passing her while she was out walking her dog. She never seemed to notice him, or his car. She was in a world of her own.

Yes, she usually was. Tired, stoned, fat. Too many children. Married to a psychopath.

That's who she's talking about, sitting there, next to the window.

One conversation on a Sunday afternoon and I probably learned more about him than in all of the others we had put together.

'How many?' I ask her.

'Three boys and a girl.' His children from his first marriage. Somebody out of the blue, in the High Street, calls out Dad to my father and – well that's why we're here, in the front room. She tells me who they are and I realise I know all of them already, apart from the one we met in the High Street, only not as anyone I'm related to. Three half-brothers and a half-sister. A weird mirror to the family I already have: three sisters and a brother, all younger than me.

'Are you going to tell the others?' The others: that's how my brothers and sisters and I always referred to each other.

'Not today, dear.'

'Not today.'

'No dear, not today.' She blinks and screws her eyes up the way she always does when she's forgotten what she's saying.

I wait. She looks down at the floor.

'You were telling me about Dad's other family.' She looks shocked. 'I don't think this was a good idea, Mum. You don't have to tell me.'

She nods a few times – that usually means she's remembered what she's doing. I sigh – she notices.

'Chris –' She sounds so sad.

'I'm sorry Mum.' I am – desperately. But sometimes I can't disguise my impatience, even if she is so much better these days. You know how sick my mother was? You wonder why I ended up being a psychiatrist?

Two years before that chat in the front room, one evening after Easter, she jumped out of her bedroom window. She stacked all the chocolate in the house, my eggs from her and from my grandmother, all of the others' eggs, in a pyramid on the bed and pulled her dressing table stool to the tall casement window facing onto the street.

Below the window was our little garden, with its tiny fishpond the size of a large silver platter. She opened the window just as I walked into the room and I watched as she stepped on to the stool. The seat of the stool reached level with the window sill, so that when she stood on it, still not having noticed me, she was able to shuffle forward and hang her toes into thin air. She was wearing her open-toed slippers.

'Mum?' I froze in the doorway. The others were at school. She sighed. 'Go and play.' She didn't turn round.

'What are you doing?' My little dog, Swipe, ran into the room.

'Nesting,' she said, squatting.

'Like a bird?' I asked, dizzy with fear. Swipe barked, his ears pricked up.

'How else?' she asked me.

I didn't know. I touched Swipe and told him to be quiet.

'What's that on the bed?' I asked, seeing the Easter eggs. Swipe barked again and jumped onto the bed.

'Eggs,' she said. 'Keep Swipe away from them.' Swipe liked sweet things.

Something was rasping, like a file on a rough piece of wood. I realised it was her breathing.

'Mum?' Swipe barked twice.

'What is it?' she started to rock, all irritable.

'Why have you done that with the eggs?' They were laid out in a triangle.

'Leave them alone,' she said. 'I'll be back before sundown.'

'Where are you going?' Swipe yapped and whimpered, lowering his ears.

'On my distant travels.' She fell forward out of the window without a sound; and as she started to fall I saw her spread her arms, as if she expected to fly. Swipe cowered like someone had hit him.

I ran to the window, shouting and pushed the stool out of the way. Mum was lying on her back, her head resting in the fishpond so her hair billowed out around her in the water. Swipe put his paws on the window ledge and strained to look down, too. There was no blood. She lay perfectly still, one leg bent at the knee with her arms by her sides, like she was sunbathing.

Somebody screamed from the other side of the road, a noise like a brake. It woke Mum up. She opened her eyes and straightened her leg. She sat up, confused like an old lady, running a hand through her wet hair.

'Chris?' She glared at me like I had my hand in the biscuit tin. 'What are you doing with the window open?'

I shut the window fast, pushing Swipe back.

If Dad hadn't been the kind of man who hadn't mown a lawn in his life Mum would probably have broken her neck. Instead, the grass on the front lawn was so long it was like a mattress.

After that she went into hospital for six months. Dad was pissed off until he started a thing with a Polish *au pair* who came to look after us.

My eyes are still closed. Oh happy memories. The women in the carriage are laughing. One of them has finished with her boyfriend. Back in the front room Mum continues to describe the family I never knew I had.

I ask her questions. *What are their names?* She tells me. *What did they do?* She tells me. One is in the army, one is in the police. One is called Stan. He had an accident, cutting off three of his toes on a boat. He lived with us for a bit when I was a baby, and gave me a giant teddy bear. He's the one we met in the High Street. Dad wasn't pleased.

Mum doesn't know what my half-sister does. *What's Dad's first wife called?* She tells me.

Then there's a pause. I remember the pause: like something passing its tipping point. She knows the question that's coming, she knows. Here it comes like a ship down its slipway: *Why did they get divorced?*

Now she looks at me as if I am ill. A lot of the time I was, of course. A lot of those pills in the medicine cabinet were for me. My mother, I might diagnose, was Munchausen's by Proxy. Induced Illness by Carer.

So she tells me, in a quiet encouraging voice, as if I am sick, or stupid:

'Dad spent time in prison *for something he didn't do.*'

She stresses that last part so carefully I feel it connect to the various threads of my life I've already managed to pull on; the inconsistencies and irrationalities of growing up around my parents that I have never been able to fathom.

Burglary? Fraud? Neither seem believable. Dad's too mad for that. I'd almost be disappointed in myself if I really thought it was something like that. No, it was something more. I wait a moment or two, staring into her glazed eyes. 'How long was he in prison for?'

'For ...' I wonder what she's thinking – counting in her head? 'Seven years.'

I don't answer. Seven years is a long time. Seven years is violent. I feel something tearing in me: the wind in the sails is too much for them.

'That's a long time.'

She licks her lip nervously. Here it comes, the story. Too bloody late, we're already at full sail.

'He helped one of his relations, his niece, who'd been in trouble after the war. She was only fifteen and she paid him back by saying he hit her.'

I knew that wasn't everything. *He hit her*. He'd hit me, so I knew he could hit.

'She was evil, Chris. Your father rescued her and she paid him back by ...' Mum's face goes white and her lip trembles. There are shadows under her eyes and I see she is making fists with her hands.

'Why was she in trouble – what happened to her in the war?'

'She was in a camp.'

'A camp?'

'Yes. Then her mother abandoned her – left her for your father to look after.'

'What happened to her?'

'Oh, she's dead.'

*

The train jolts, throwing me out of my thoughts. Outside the carriage, the bushes beside the line seem to be passing behind me. In the distance the trees on the horizon somehow appear to be moving ahead as though the landscape's stirring, revolving.

I'm on a rescue mission. Helping someone out.

I look at the picture of the Maria Tomaseli. I'm heading towards a murder. I watch the fields; a narrow road cutting through; a flock of sheep, staring.

Whatever you're trying to avoid, it's probably already happening. Who told me that? I wait – will there be an answer? Will I hear one? Or was that ... it feels distant. The idea of me being in London, older, fatter, greyer ... in Harley Street with Kay.

Kate's dead.

Those thoughts, which don't make sense, and my voice, my older voice, they evaporate: steam like the dampness I feel around me as my clothes dry out from the rain.

I picture Blanca, my supervisor, the afternoon before I left London for Pisa. Russian, apparently made out of iron and slate, our relationship is anything but comfortable. Why do I insist on working with her? She understands me, somehow. I've worked with her since I started training as a psychotherapist and she talked about my first patients with me at a run-down hospital in Dartford.

She was sitting in the chair, which was the same place I imagined she sat when she was practising as an analyst. A broad low couch covered in coarse blankets and Ottoman cushions, modelled on Freud's, I assumed, came between us like a coffee table. The seat she provided for me – an old wooden thing with intricate carving on the spars at the back and graceful, dark legs – stood more to the side of the couch than at the end of it.

I explained why I was going to Italy and she made the noise like a strange bird that she sometimes made after I said something she felt a need to challenge. She did it a lot. I've never quite pinned the root of the sound down, but once, when I saw a couple of starlings running along the ground and thought I recognised some sort of prehistoric motion, I got close.

'It's absurd,' she said.

That was all she said, before sitting back in her psychoanalytic majesty. Her chair, I once noticed, was distinctly lower than mine. She was a small woman, so a man my size would always look down on her in conversations.

I had no real idea about Blanca's past other than that she was from Russia, that she read the *Morning Star* in English when she was a student, as it was the only newspaper she could get where she lived, and that she worked with refugees. But I often felt that she might have had some connection, at some time, to the military.

I didn't have much choice other than to agree with her, anyway. I'd already recognised in myself that something I was doing was absurd.

'But that couldn't be entirely it, could it?'

'Of course not,' she replied, looking out of the window, onto a large overgrown garden. The lawn was mown but the bushes and trees along either side and at the end, where there was some kind of a small wood, seemed to do as they pleased.

'There's a feeling that you can right an injustice,' she said.

I was defensive. 'And you're thinking that I'm caught up perhaps in something to do with my father?'

She laughed and shook her head like a big cat trying to slip a collar; then stopped abruptly and looked directly at me.

'Of course you're caught up in something to do with your father. We both know that. But I'm surprised *you*, and I have to say *you*, because I have a great respect for you,' she moved on from saying this so quickly I was barely able to register it, pausing perhaps only a fraction of a beat, 'I'm most surprised that *you* would ever be content with such a storybook formulation.'

'Sorry?'

'You heard me.' She sounded impatient. 'Your father suffers an injustice so you feel there is something in you prone to right a wrong.'

'I was thinking something like that,' I told her.

'Chris. If you did *not* have that impulse, you would possibly be ...' she searched for a word, 'inhuman. What you're doing is absurd, but that part of it feels to me entirely reasonable. You believe that you're somehow complicit ...' She stopped.

I wanted her to go on.

'You have to work the rest out.' She looked out of the window again. 'It feels to me as if there's something else going on here.'

'What do you mean?' How could she say that, based on only what she'd heard?

'I mean that in your case, Christopher, there are many places for things to hide.'

'So you're saying I shouldn't go?'

'How could I say that? Simon will, of course, have a big problem with it.'

'I know,' I answered.

'You see, you have thought about that. And you've thought for some time about your fractious relationship with Simon. Anyway, we've talked about that.' She sighed. 'Make sure this is not a very elaborate way of doing *that:* leaving him. Make sure that you are most aware of what you do not know.'

'What I don't know?'

'Yes. And be extremely careful.'

CHAPTER 15
PISA – CAMAIORE, 1986

The train's slowing. I check my watch: we must be most of the way there.

We stop and several people get on: a group of men who glance at the two young women, still talking away in their emphatic, loping style and then head for the other end of the carriage; an older woman with what looks like her grandson; a little girl and her mother – and through the open doors I see another woman standing staring in. Our eyes meet. I know her – do I know her? She looks familiar and a name comes to me: Kay. But I don't know anybody called Kay.

She stands there, drawing on a cigarette, the hem of her summer dress dancing around her calves as another train pulls away from the next platform. I can't read her expression; although our eyes have met I can't say whether she has seen me. She has – she nods, throws the cigarette down, smiles, steps into the carriage and comes towards me. Yes, she knows me.

'Chris,' she says, taking the seat beside me. She puts her hand on my leg and kisses me on the cheek. I don't know what to say. The scene feels so ordinary, and so impossible.

I look at the men chatting, nodding their heads gently to the rhythm of the train as it rattles on towards Camaiore. The little girl and her mother are facing me, either side of a table halfway down the carriage. 'Kay,' I say.

She's gone. Who is she?

The little girl's looking at me, then into the space beside me. She looks back at me, and then at her mother. She whispers something in her mother's ear. Maybe: that man's imagining things. The mother fans herself – it's very hot – looks at me sharply and then also into the space beside me. She sighs and shakes her head, nods at me, realising I have seen her, and scolds her daughter. The little girl looks down at the table sadly, turning over the pages of a magazine her mother lays out for her. She looks up at me and then back at the magazine.

The two young women keep talking. I lose track of their voices without realising. Without my knowing it, they're gone.

*

The train arrives shortly after midday. The carriage is hot but perhaps because it has been moving, or maybe because I've been still, it feels twice as hot outside. Almost unbearable. The station's small and I leave it quickly, ahead of the other passengers.

Dogs. There are lots of them in Camaiore, sleeping under trees while their owners stand chatting, leads hanging loose and the dogs maybe wishing all the people weren't there at all so they could wander home and sit somewhere they wouldn't be disturbed until night-time.

It feels like a small place, a lot of people riding around on old-fashioned bicycles, old buildings, nothing new, as if nothing that's happened in the last hundred years has mattered too much – let alone the murders. People look calm.

I stop under a tree. I don't know anything about trees, but it had some beautiful leaves like the old eucalyptus tree I'd had at home. The leaves were like confetti. When I sat under it I saw stars, the bright spaces between the leaves.

I know where I want to go: there's a café John visited in Camaiore – one of the last places he went before he disappeared. It's on the main street, opposite a church and I can see the spire towering over the other buildings, all low, squat, as though they are kneeling. I walk down the first street I see heading towards it. There's a market on and it's crowded. People bump up against me. It's hot, really hot. As though I'm wearing an overcoat.

The first thing I see: there's a painting of the owners hanging behind the bar. I go in, take a table next to the window onto the street and look around me. Straight away I see the two young women from the train sitting at the back of the café; I feel myself go still. They're writing postcards. I want to say hello, but they wouldn't have a clue who I am. Funny: I noticed them, they've stayed with me but they wouldn't know me.

A waiter brings me my coffee and I sip from it, discreetly watching them. There are a few other people here but nobody between us. They've laid things out on their table: a camera, a map, a book. One of the women puts her pen down and stares at the book. She's thin, lively looking, as if she could be an athlete, a runner. I've always been attracted to women like that – nothing like the women I grew up with. Her face is relaxed, firm, narrow; she's got dark hair, tied into a kind of Japanese-looking knot: one that seems to keep reaching up, like a lotus. Maybe she's tall. She reaches out for the book and there's something so graceful about how she moves; I want to think of an animal, something like a deer or an antelope, but for some reason I think of a tree. The branches of a willow, strong and supple. I can't tell for sure as she's sitting with her legs stretched under the table.

Her hand hovers over the book but she decides not to pick it up and leans down to her side to the side to get something out of her bag. As she does so her black shirt opens up and for a moment I see the curve of her breasts.

She catches my eye, smiles and I start, spilling my coffee. It runs down my fingers onto my wrists. Embarrassed, I put the coffee cup down and wipe my hands on a serviette. She stands up, tugging at the shoulder of her top, pulling softly so the material draws a little tighter around her chest. I can't stop myself: I smile back.

Maybe something's conspiring to help me: the clink of glasses behind the bar, the smell of coffee under my nose. Whatever it is, I'm grateful she's noticed me.

Then she's beside me, at my table.

'Do you have a light?'

And I'm aware, for some reason I can't describe, of her heart. I find my eyes resting below her breast, where her heart is, beating slowly, and I imagine fingers stroking my own chest, circling my heart.

'I think so.'

I reach into my jacket pocket. I know I don't have a light but I reach in anyway. I've got a light, cold and hard. I feel the rough metal wheel with my thumb as I take it out. I stare at it. It's the lighter I remember seeing on Semproni's desk.

'Thank you.'

I wonder how I ended up with it my pocket, and I look at her. Sometimes I'll just catch sight of a woman, or hear her voice – sometimes it's that – I don't even have to see her; she might be on the other side of a restaurant or serving someone in a shop, but then I have to have her look at me. And that's easy, I look at her until she does, then I smile, and whatever it is I do when I smile, most of the time the woman smiles back.

I realise our fingers have brushed. She has the lighter although I don't remember giving it to her; I've been distracted.

'Are you a local?' she asks in a London accent, which surprises me. How had she sounded on the train? I can't remember that either.

The waiter comes by and says something in Italian. I don't understand. The woman answers in Italian, without looking at him, smiling at me. She says something about me, I'm sure – probably something about me being English, and she sounds very much an Italian.

I tell her no, I'm not a local. I'm here on business.

And the waiter goes to the jukebox beside the bar, the kind that plays records, little black seven-inch vinyl ones. He puts in a coin and presses a button. Click. Clunk. A metal arm lifts a disk, rotates it, drops it onto a silver rod in the middle of a glittering turntable, already spinning, the size of a dinner plate. Another arm rises, shifts inwards and descends onto the record. There's a crackling noise, way too loud – and then there's the Ronettes, just as loud. *Mean Streets: 'Be My Baby'.*

The woman's grinning. 'Do you like it?'

'Yes, I do.'

'I thought you might.'

'You asked him to put it on?'

'I think you look like Harvey Keitel.'

'I think I'm taller than him.' I have always thought I look like Harvey Keitel.

'So I imagine you know his films.'

'Yes I do.'

She sits down in the seat opposite me. 'You're wondering about my heart, aren't you?'

'What?'

'My heart.'

I feel ridiculous. Crazy. I look back at her friend, still writing postcards, and then out into the street. People are walking by as if nothing in particular's going on.

The waiter's cleaning glasses.

Be My Baby. The music's like crushed sugar, coffee, a window misting over with somebody else's breath.

The woman touches my wrist. My hand trembles – just a little.

'My heart?' Her hand's cold.

I don't say anything.

'Everybody notices my heart. It's my best feature but nobody ever says so, because they can't believe it's my heart. They think it's something else.'

'If they did think it was your heart do you think they'd tell you?'

She takes hold of my wrist with her cold hand and moves her frozen finger over my palm. 'You'd like to look more like Robert de Niro wouldn't you?'

'I think I would.' I've always wanted to look more like Robert de Niro.

'I don't think Robert de Niro would notice my heart.' She places my hand on her chest below her breast. 'There.' She draws my fingers up so I feel the weight of her breast.

I can feel her heart beating, like something all of itself. A little creature.

'What business brings you here?'

'Medical.'

Her eyes narrow. 'Body or mind?'

I laugh. She doesn't and I stop. She sits there with the Ronettes playing, calm, very calm, but not like anything I'm used to. 'Nobody's asked me that before.'

'Nobody's got a heart like me.'

'I see.'

We're silent, then I speak. 'I'm a psychiatrist.'

'I see.' Her voice was rhythmical, languorous, like rain that had been falling all day.

'I'm also a psychotherapist.'

'Do you think I would be talking to you like this if you were just a psychiatrist?' She looks at her watch, a little black thing like a bracelet. 'What are you doing today?'

'I'm working.'

'Then we can see each other this evening.'

I didn't know what to say, so I don't say anything.

'Come to our hotel, on the market square, next to the cinema. We'll be there from six.'

'Both of you?'

She smiles – a kind of smile I really can't read. 'Of course. Asha's special, too.'

'Asha?'

'Yes, Asha.'

I glance onto the street, notice an old man walking past cradling a black cat in his arms, talking to the animal, then I look back at her.

'Look at that,' I say.

She's looking. She thanks me, smiles again, returns to her table with her friend and starts writing postcards again, head down, as if I'm not there. Her friend, Asha, looks up at me once, blinking, as if she doesn't see me at all. And she doesn't.

So, I get up and go back into the street. In the sun my strange little meeting soon falls away from me – like dust on something you take out of an old wardrobe, a jacket, and you put it on, and you wonder why you'd hide the jacket away like that.

I follow the road away from the church, feeling as if there are sparks in me: a little comet. I stand in the sun, take my Walkman out of my bag, swap my tape for the one Simon made, clip it to my belt and plug in the headphones. It doesn't take me long to find the place on the tape where John follows Christina through Camaiore from the café – where to? Her gallery. The place he went to buy his stock. As I listen, caught up in the sound of Louise's voice, I follow in his footsteps like someone at an art exhibition or sightseeing. There's something about being able to do what he did.

LOUISE
John started after her but the street was thick with people.

Today there are people – not so many, though. This doesn't feel crowded. Today, whatever the reason, it's not so busy.

LOUISE
She hurried through a group of children and vanished into the crowd. He ran on, straining to see over other people's heads and caught sight of the top of her head bobbing

ahead of him. Pushing in between people, he caught up with her where the street joined the town's main square, and he reached out –

'Christina?'

A cyclist darted between them, nearly knocking him off his feet.

She was gone.

He looked for her, but something else caught his attention. Down an alley barely wide enough for anyone to walk through without their shoulders touching the edges he saw two dogs, sitting dead still.

That alley? It must be – dark and narrow. I stand at the end of it, peering in, imagining the dogs. Then I see the dogs.

LOUISE

Were they the same pair he'd seen sleeping under a tree when he'd parked his car in the main square? They looked like a couple of statues, so still it was hard to believe that they had hearts.

Two statues: they have hearts, beating like this, like mine, as I stand here.

LOUISE

Behind him, in the square, there was bustle and noise; around the dogs, in that narrow alley, there was space and stillness.

Then, for no reason that he could see, they stood up and stretched.

They flick their tails, making small movements. One small dog and one larger, which twitches its ear.

LOUISE
They padded away – then they stopped. The smaller one looked back, catching his eye. John took a step and the dogs moved on.

I stop; they stop. I follow and they move. This is how we go, down the alley to a dirty little street running along the back of some broken-down houses. My steps echo and scuff. You come to Camaiore, you wouldn't want to come this way: weeds between the cobblestones; cans and paper bags. Small, dusty back yards separated from each other by wooden fences – rotting. I stop. They stop. Already I don't know where I am, but I have an idea of somewhere I'm heading. Somebody's waiting for me.

LOUISE
They reached another alley, almost as narrow as the first –

This one: a little wider, dark, always in shadow. I put my palm against the brick and feel how cold it is. The woman in the bar. I think of her hand – and I think: I don't know her name. Asha, that's her friend. But who was she? Did she tell me? Why didn't I ask? This feels like – it seems: I'm going backwards.

LOUISE
The dogs started moving differently: prowling, low to the ground as if they were stalking something. They stopped. He stopped.

I'm facing a door and the dogs are sitting still, panting, staring at it. I *know* this is Christina's door. I inch closer. The door's black. It's battered and split. I reach out and touch it: it's warm, as though the sun's been shining on it – although the sun can't ever shine down here.

The dogs stare at me. Their hackles rise and they growl, a rough, terrible sound – like a machine, like a drill. I pull my hand away and they fall silent, looking at the door again. They're waiting. They're waiting and – something happens, like a breath, and they trot away. I find my heart beating hard, and I hadn't realised; as time passes, it slows.

LOUISE
He knocked. Nobody answered. He waited, then knocked again.

Nobody. I turn the handle, slowly until it clicks. I pull. Nothing. So I rattle it. 'Christina?'

LOUISE
No answer. He stood there and he waited. Then he went back to the café, to Kate, and he told her what had happened.
    'What did she do that for?' asked Kate.
    He told her he didn't know.

I press stop, still standing in front of the door, take off my headphones and wonder what to do next. I look down at the concrete under my feet. A few weeks ago John stood there. I hesitate, then I knock on the door again.
    Still no answer. I turn it and push – and it opens.
    It opens as if something about it is broken; like I'm lifting back the wing of a great, dead bird. I call inside.
    'Hello?'

Nobody replies. It's dark and I smell something damp, almost woody, like wet leaves. It's too dark to see inside. I find a light switch and flick it up and down a few times. No luck. Am I going in? I call out again, then step into the darkness, holding the door open. The woody smell's stronger; after a few moments my eyes adjust. There's another door a few feet in front of me. If I want to go there I have to let go of the one I'm holding. What is this? A hall? Coat hooks, peeling paint. Concrete floor.

I let go and walk towards the other door: three, may be four steps is all – but after two I'm in the dark. Completely in the dark and even though I know the sane thing would be to keep moving ... I stop. I reach out in front of me, but there's nothing there. Nothing there yet: one step, two step. There: hardness. I push, hoping, and it swings half-open. Light floods over me: windows, glass. The sky.

I open the door and go in.

Tall wooden cabinets lining the walls, glass-fronted, the kind you display little objects in, and as if they should have been somewhere much bigger. They're all empty. Every single one of them. Whatever was inside them, it's all gone.

The bare floorboards creak as I step on them. Ahead of me: that's the front of the gallery. Little square windows, one of them smashed. There's a small stone on the floor, and pieces of glass. Under the broken window there's a damp patch. I go over, squat down and realise it's the source of the woody smell. And I smell something else – cigarettes. There's a half-smoked Silk Cut crushed on the floor inside the front door. Beside that there's a pile of letters. I leaf through them: days of unopened mail.

Looking at the cigarette I guess someone else was here since it was locked up – someone who's sorted the post.

Only it isn't locked up. The back door's open.

What else is there? An empty Coke can on top of one of the cabinets; a crumpled paper bag next to it. This feels still and airless. Really still, like water on a lake on a grey, windless day. Still, but not peaceful.

I don't like it.

Something's happened here which has left a stain – and all of a sudden I'm thinking of something I read about, a bay somewhere, high on the Alaskan coast. There were photographs. At one end of the bay there was a glacier: a wall of sheer ice and rock hanging over the still, blue water. Around the edge of the lake there were young, short pine trees nothing like the great, barbed giants further away from the shore.

One morning a couple of fishermen out alone in the bay heard a noise like thunder. Looking towards the glacier at the far end of the bay they thought they saw steam, or white smoke. Then, out of nowhere, a wave over a hundred metres high surged from the horizon towards them. Helpless, they felt the wave lift them high over the trees, as though they were flying. It carried them out of the bay before dropping them, as abruptly as it had picked them up, far out at sea.

The glacier had crumbled, throwing up a wave the height of a block of flats which tore up the trees on the edge of the bay, washing everything away. It did that every few decades, leaving its print.

That's how it feels. Something's stripped everything away. I look up at the empty cabinets, towering over me and I feel uneasy. I really shouldn't be here.

Tapping.

It must be coming from the room over this one. Something moving slowly, as if somebody's walking ... tapping like heels – more like clicking. I look around me, at the cabinets;

back at the door where I came in. As I do so I see the handle turn. Silently, it turns – and then turns back, as if whoever's on the other side has changed their mind.

I call out: 'Hello?' The tapping stops.

A moment passes, then it starts again, even more slowly than before. I walk to the door and pull at the handle. It opens easily.

The door to the alley's half-open, propped with a brick.

My heart's beating, almost sucking on me. It doesn't want to be here either; a child sucking on its thumb. I go back into the gallery, leaving the second door open. No more tapping.

I can see back out into the alley.

I wait there five minutes, looking up at the ceiling, and out of the back door onto the alley. Nothing moves; I see nobody. So I get out of the place.

I think about going straight back to Pisa, but there's the woman I met in the café – and there's the Villa Inghilterra. I go back to the main square and take a taxi to the Villa Inghilterra, thinking about where I've just been.

CHAPTER 16
CAMAIORE, 1986

And I'm still half-thinking about it when my taxi pulls up outside the Villa Inghilterra. The other half of me has been trying to catch a glimpse of the place since my taxi turned off the main road and started bumping its way down the uneven drive to where we are now. Even that turn from the main road seemed to be hidden. Suddenly we were veering to the left, across the carriageway, ignoring a truck that had to brake, horn blaring, and then we were climbing. I don't remember our speed changing once.

So I'm here. The Villa Inghilterra.

I pay the driver and step out into the sun. It's so bright I need to look down – and that doesn't help much because the white-ish chalky dust on the drive seems to catch the sun as strongly as ever, reflecting it back into my face. It feels as if I'm in front of a fire. There's a dark shape, though. I step into it, dark and cool: a shadow. The shadow of the clock tower. It's late in the afternoon and the shadows are starting to lengthen, but this one's already long. A straight, dark neck leading all the way to the base of the tower.

I walk into it, looking up at the scaffolding; the tarpaulin wrapped around the top. This thing looms. I hadn't realised. This tower towers. I think about the wave that washed through the bay in Alaska; about the deep, green water and the wave rising above it.

Next to it this place, the villa, seems to shrink. It's very old, a Renaissance villa with its flat roof, arches and beautiful dimensions, but next to the tower it shrinks to nothing.

I'm scared – am I? Why am I here? I'm here to help Louise.

Louise.

I'm thinking of the canvas that fell from the wardrobe at Wasing. The painting with the strip scratched from it.

And I think of Blanca again and remember, remember it specifically, the first time I managed to talk to her about how turned on I'd felt in the room with one of my patients: V, a young woman. She was ten years younger than me, very pretty, and she said something to me that seemed completely unconnected with sex. Suddenly, though, I became aware that the space between us felt as if it was writhing, alive. My eyes shifted to the door, and she noticed. We were sitting face to face.

'What is it?' she asked.

I looked back and the way I looked back caught her attention even more.

'What is it?' she asked again.

When I told Blanca, she asked me, first of all, what the woman had been talking about. Of course I couldn't remember. So Blanca asked me if it was the first time I'd felt strong sexual feelings when I was with a client. I'd hesitated, because I realised, and I couldn't believe I'd only realised that then, that I couldn't remember feeling any such thing.

I could remember noticing that I found patients attractive, men and women, I told her.

'And in doing so,' Blanca cut in, as she was always liable to do, 'you were telling yourself to feel nothing. You say you felt nothing towards them?'

'I thought,' I went with my first thought, even though I couldn't really say whether it was true or not, 'maybe I feel colder towards them.'

'Cold? Towards the ones you find attractive?'

'Colder,' I corrected her.

'I'm surprised,' she said. 'Somebody has missed something.' That, of course, was what she said when she believed there was something I needed to discuss with my therapist. I think sometimes Blanca wished she was my therapist rather than my supervisor. Maybe that's what she'd missed.

'I don't have an analyst any more,' I reminded her. After finishing my training and qualifying, I'd ended my therapy as quickly as I could.

'So you wanted to what? what did you want?' Blanca asked.

I couldn't say.

'You felt aroused?'

'Yes,' I said. But even as I said so, I couldn't be sure. I felt something uncomfortable. Maybe I felt aroused, maybe I felt appalled. 'I felt something uncomfortable,' I said, 'something to be ashamed of.'

'Have you ever wanted to sleep with me?' she asked.

I couldn't stop myself from laughing.

She tilted her head to one side. I imagined kissing her neck and her taking hold of me, holding my head in both hands and pushing me away, her eyes cool and deep and then pushing me back in my chair and standing over me. She slapped me. I felt my cock go hard. She hit me again and I tasted blood trickling from my lip and she unbuttoned her shirt and showed me her breasts. Her thin body and her breasts like two fists. And she hit me again.

'I can see it isn't that simple,' she said.

My mind fixed on what I'd imagined, and I fell silent. After some time I realised I didn't know how long I'd been silent. I was sweating.

Blanca sat there, suddenly gentle, and I had no idea how she had transformed herself so quickly into somebody quite as soft and caring as the person in front of me.

'It's all right,' she said, her voice as quiet as I'd ever heard it.

My face was trembling. There were pins and needles in my feet. My hands felt cold and numb. I realised how quickly I was breathing – twice as fast as normal. My fingers were stiff. 'What's happening to me?'

She sat still and nodded. 'It's all right,' she said. 'You're very frightened.'

I saw that my fingers had begun to bend back on themselves, to twist, as if I wanted to grip something but I was gripping the wrong way. My heart was going to stop: a car hitting a wall.

'You're very frightened,' she said. 'You're very scared.' She paused. 'You're as frightened as you can be, but you're going to be all right.' She reached across and gently placed a hand on my wrist.

I think I might have flinched if I'd felt her touch me, but I couldn't feel a thing – and I'd never have imagined her touching me like *that*. Her finger shook as she touched me, my trembling passing into her.

'My hands,' I said.

'Your hands will be fine. You maybe want to strangle somebody. Perhaps me. But there's no need.' She smiled. 'Your mind won't let you strangle anyone.'

I'd seen her smile before, but always it had seemed at my expense. Now she was smiling like my mother.

'All I would say, of course, is to remember what you are seeing.'

I must have shaken my head. She raised her eyebrows.

'There's nothing more instructive than an experience of powerlessness.'

Maybe I nodded.

'If you were an alcoholic, this is the kind of thing which might lead you not to drink. As you are a psychotherapist I would say ... maybe you don't just want to help people.'

I laughed. She did too: gently but powerfully, like a queen would laugh. I felt myself relaxing. We sat like that, her hand gently resting on my wrist, and I noticed how warm her hand was. I closed my eyes and felt myself getting warmer.

Perhaps half an hour later, long beyond the end of the session, eventually, exhausted, I asked her: 'What happened?'

She leaned back in her seat. 'You were shocked,' she said. 'You were very frightened and you froze. Like animals do. Like people do. Perhaps if you think about that, that will help you connect with what was going on when you were sitting with a woman and you felt cold towards her.'

'I don't feel cold.'

She smiled again.

I got up to leave.

'And what was the young woman talking about?' she asked. 'Can you remember now?'

'Peaches,' I said.

She smiled. And then she laughed.

*

I walk in through the main entrance and ring the bell at reception. A pretty, older-looking woman in a summer dress appears from a room at the back and says hello. She's called Mrs Smith.

She says good afternoon in Italian and checks me over quickly, noticing my bag, maybe wondering why I don't have a suitcase.

'Good afternoon,' I reply in English, realising I have no idea what I'm going to say.

'How can I help?' she asks in English. She sounds as though she is English; her voice is soft, maybe hopeful. A little sad.

I hesitate.

'Do you have a room booked?' Her eyes are red. Perhaps she's been crying. I can see her make-up's been carefully applied. Underneath I think she may be very pale.

'No, I don't. I'm working with the police on the France case.'

'Are you a police officer?' She sounds far more frosty and folds her arms. 'Can I see your identification?'

'I'm not a police officer.'

She leans forward and hits the bell on the desk three times with the flat of her hand. 'Adam? Adam. There's another one here.'

A noble-looking man, maybe ten years older than her, appears from a back room, glaring like an old lion. 'What is it?' His voice is deep and clear. He's old but he still commands.

I smile back gently, which seems to make both of them glare even harder.

'I'm a doctor,' I say quickly. 'I'm a doctor.' I feel myself cling to the phrase.

They soften at the same time, but still look at me suspiciously.

'Another one?' asks the woman.

'Yes,' said the man. 'Another one? I told the other chap, what do we need a doctor for?'

'I'm a psychiatrist.'

'So was he. So he said he was.' Mr Smith shakes his head. 'Do you have any kind of identification?'

I show them my passport and point to my profession: *psychiatrist*. It gets more respect than *psychotherapist*.

'Well, what do you want?' asks Mrs Smith.

'I've been asked to think about John and Kate France.'

'The other chap, then,' asks Mrs Smith, 'who was he?'

'I don't know.'

'He was English,' he says. 'Pushy, with a beard. About your age. Very pushy.'

'Smoked like a chimney,' says the woman.

'Simon?' I ask.

'Simon. That's right. Yes, he said his name – can't remember his second name – but his first name was Simon,' says the man. 'You know him?'

'Yes, I do.'

They wait for me to say something else, but I don't.

'Actually,' I begin, 'I'd like a room here, please, if you have one?'

Mrs Smith frowns and says they don't have one.

'Steady on,' her husband replies, holding up his hand. 'Steady on, dear, he's only doing his job and,' he speaks more slowly, 'he wants a *room*.'

Mrs Smith sighs. 'I'm sorry, this has been terribly unpleasant for us.'

'And it certainly hasn't been good for business,' Mr Smith says. 'Smith,' he says. 'This is my wife, Mrs Smith.'

I greet them both.

'I really am sorry,' says Mrs Smith, unfolding her arms, a red ridge running up her forearms. Her face is flushed. 'This has been horrible.'

'I can imagine.'

'I have no idea,' she says, turning to her husband, 'no idea what happened.'

'Neither of us has.' He adds, pausing: 'No idea at all. They were a lovely couple. He was ... intense. Wasn't he?' He turns to his wife.

She nods and tells me how she saw John sitting outside the tower the morning he and Kate had arrived. 'But I took it – he looked happy enough – I took it he was soaking up the whole thing ... getting married.'

'Yes, people do that,' says Mr Smith. 'When you do a job like ours you get used to seeing people react to things ... in their ways. Sometimes peculiar. Sometimes people like to go off on their own. Sometimes they walk about a bit. Sometimes they sit and read.'

'Sometimes they sleep,' adds Mrs Smith.

'Did you tell this to the other psychiatrist?'

'No,' he said. 'He never asked. He came and went, didn't stay, poked around, lit a few cigarettes, half-smoked them, had tea on the terrace and then ... he was off.'

Perhaps the cigarette stubbed out on the floor in Camaiore was Simon's.

'You can take your pick from the rooms,' says Mrs Smith, showing me the rows of keys on hooks behind him. 'All of them are empty.'

'I'll take the honeymoon suite.'

'The honeymoon suite.' She picks up a pen and holds it a few moments, the tip hovering over a form. 'OK. The one they had.'

'Yes please.'

She asks me my name. I tell her; we complete the form together, filling in the name of the room as if it were any other.

I sign the form and put my name in the register.

'We're planning to close down for a few days and take a break,' she says. 'Wait for things to die down. How long do you think you'll be staying?'

'Just a night.'

'Just tonight. So we'll be going away,' says her husband. 'But, if you want another night ...' He pauses. 'Maybe we can wait. What do you want to do while you're here? Do you want to ask us anything?'

I don't know.

'I think we'd like to talk about it. Maybe tomorrow, though.'

'Of course.'

Mr Smith takes a large key from one of the hooks behind him and walks me in silence to my room. It seems a long way. When we get there I glance at the door. I touch it.

'Brand new,' says Mr Smith. He puts the key in the lock and turns it. A small click. He shows me in, a look on his face as if he wishes he hadn't said anything, and I have in my mind's eye a scene of smashed and broken things. Torn sheets and empty drawers; a ripped mattress and gashed pillows.

Nothing like it. The room is neat and well ordered: the bed newly made; a white blanket drawn tight over the sheets; a water jug and a folded towel on the dressing table. A portrait of a young woman wearing a necklace; a gold book hanging from the necklace – and *she* catches my eye.

You, I think. You. Who am I thinking of? I have a strange memory of a woman in the snow and somehow, as if I am looking at her from above, I beckon her towards me. I'm knocking on something – knocking on glass. Tapping, and she sees me ... and it's gone. I'm looking at the portrait and I realise Mr Smith has taken me by the arm.

'Are you all right?' He looks worried. 'You look as though you've seen a ghost.'

I squint at him. For a moment his face seems blurred. 'So do you.' My head's pounding. He helps me to sit down on the bed. 'I'll be OK,' I say. 'Just the sun or something.' I look at the portrait again. I imagine Kate sitting where I am, thinking the same. 'Tell me,' I ask, 'did this room end up in a mess?'

'A mess?'

I'm holding something in mind as I speak to him. K, the Jack France book.

'After John France disappeared.'

He folds his arms. 'Mess is a kind way of putting it. The room was ruined. We had to put it together again from scratch.'

'That picture?'

'Not that. She survived the storm – somehow.'

We stare at her together.

'Who is she?'

'I've no idea.'

He unfolds his arms and excuses himself, closing the door behind him.

I lie back on the bed, happier knowing it isn't the one Kate and John spent the night in, but still aware there's room for somebody else beside me. I shift towards the wall, as if to give them more space. What did I do that for? I look to my side, imagine Kate doing the same, seeing the note on the pillow, reading it and thinking – what?

She'd been writing letters to a dead man as if he were alive.

I stare at the ceiling. I can understand that. Dead writers keep telling you things, don't they? As long as you keep reading them.

I think about the crazy business with the letters, lose myself in it ... and then I come back out of it realising I'm looking at the portrait of the woman again. Who's this woman I'm staring at, with her necklace and her book; a picture of a face I'll never know? Someone like Kate who I'll never really see.

I think about this room getting turned over and I think about the letters. The confusion between Kate and John. I lie there quietly, thinking, and a story comes to me, a famous one: Poe's *Purloined Letter*. A story about a love letter. One belonging to a queen.

The scenes arrive in pieces, each one almost like a letter I open in between glancing around at the portrait, the pillow, the walls and the doors.

A letter belonging to the queen has been stolen by her chief minister – a letter revealing details of an affair that she's having.

I see the minister come into the royal boudoir and with his lynx eye, I imagine his lynx eye, notices the letter on a table. Only the address is showing. The queen is with her husband, from whom she has earlier tried to hide the letter. The minister understands what is going on, the delicate balance between what is being hidden and what's on show, and puts a similar looking letter down on the table next to the queen's. He goes about his normal business and then, as he leaves, picks up the queen's letter. She's horrified but there's nothing she can do. The king is beside her.

The minister uses the letter to blackmail the queen – I see this, a plump, ugly man taunting her – so she asks her prefect of police to search for the letter and retrieve it.

He fails.

I see him failing, turning the minister's rooms upside down.

He calls in a private detective, Dupin.

Dupin believes that the letter must be close to hand, as the blackmail threat would be worthless if the minister isn't able to produce the letter almost immediately.

Dupin. A combination of *flâneur* and Victorian man of duty; Holmes on the threshold of an opium den. The police chief and his men have searched behind the wallpaper, under carpets, even inside the furniture.

But Dupin realises that because the minister is a poet the prefect underestimates him. What does a poet know about anything?

When Dupin finds the letter, it's in front of everybody's noses, but disguised.

I see Dupin take it from the minister's card rack and replace it with his own copy.

I stare at the pillow beside me and feel very close to something. They say the truth is out there – maybe it's a lot closer to hand. If only I knew what I was looking for.

I think of Blanca. If only I knew what I was looking for *or why I was looking for it.*

Oh. The bed's soft. It's hot and I'm sweating. I rearrange my clothes and another scene comes to me.

I'm a boy and my father asks me to fetch something for him. It's in the garage where he stores his junk in chaos. I start to sweat because unless I'm very lucky I never find what my father asks me to get him. He sits in his velour armchair in the front room eating grapes, spitting out the skins and heaping them into my hands to carry to the bin in the kitchen, describing what it is he wants in between my journeys, why he wants it and what he's going to do with it.

I go to the garage. This time I remember what it is he wants: to begin with – a cutting tool for copper pipes. There'll be other things. He wants to change the place where the washing machine stands. Sometimes I manage to forget even before I reach the back door, in the kitchen.

I go out and open the garage door. The handle's an old Bakelite knob which wobbles as I turn it. Inside it smells of fruit. It's the summer and Dad buys boxes of oranges and peaches from the market at London Bridge. He stacks them inside the door and sometimes eats them. Sometimes the fruit rots – and that's what I smell: rotting fruit, too sweet, like alcohol.

It isn't dark yet but I still need the light – an old black switch which looks ready to catch fire. The bulb hanging from the ceiling lights up and I start to look. Where?

'Inside ze garage,' he said, Polishly.

Inside the garage are so many tools, packages and pieces of machinery I know I have barely any chance of finding what I'm looking for. Searching methodically is less likely to help me than randomly lifting things, rummaging in boxes and opening doors. Sometimes I feel that if I let myself get close enough to my father's horrible mind I can predict what he's done with the thing he wants. Today ... I look ... and no luck. I look for ten, maybe fifteen minutes, my heart beating more quickly and the sick feeling in my stomach becoming heavier with every *nothing* I find.

Nothing.

Nothing.

Nothing.

Nothing.

Nothing.

Nothing.

Nothing.

I go back inside slowly, full of dread. He's watching TV in his underpants, hairy and fat like an animal. He looks at me and I want to die.

'Wat eez the problem.'

My head aches, sleepiness drawing over me. Everything feels tired, closed and impossible.

'I can't find it.'

'Wat you mean?' he snaps, ears twitching, unblinking eyes fixed on mine, his fat body tensing. No shirt, no trousers, no socks. Those summers were so hot.

'I can't find it.'

He screeches, his voice growing shrill, his face colouring up and contorting: 'Fochen lazy bastard.' He slams his hand down on the coffee table. 'I count to ten.'

I run back to the garage scared senseless, waiting for him to explode. And everyone blames me for it – his shrieking and shouting; his screaming that he'll kill me. 'Bastard, you are not my son, I fochen kill you.' Only very rarely did he hit me, and that was usually a surprise. The shouting, he knew, wasn't going to land him back in prison.

I still can't find what he wants so he jumps up and gets it himself. He finds it straight away. After all, *he* put it there. He knew where it was. He tells me, stuffing it in my face: it was right under my nose.

*

I sit up. I'm breathing heavily and I feel sick. I get up and turn the picture on the wall round. There's my bag. I get out the Walkman, put on my headphones and forward the tape almost to the very end, where Louise describes how Kate disappeared.

I press play.

LOUISE

We were walking through town, the day after John disappeared. It was late afternoon and we'd spent the morning with the police. Kate was nervous.

We were walking.

She kept thinking John was going to turn up. Once or twice I saw her look around as if he might be right beside her. And then she looked puzzled. She looked really sad.

We went as far as the square, without saying anything to each other. And then she saw the cinema. There was a poster outside for *Butch Cassidy and the Sundance Kid*. It was John's favourite film.

I asked if she wanted to see it.

She said she did.

We were on the balcony at the back, Kate on my left, a couple of rows back from the door. There were other people in there. The film had already started. Butch and Sundance lay watching some men riding after them. I remember was a man wearing a white hat. I remember the sound of the horses' hooves over the hard ground.*

---

* Originally I thought about including lines from a transcript of the scene where Butch and Sundance jump from a great height into the river below. For this particular book, though, which is about ghosts and haunting, I think it's better if I suggest you go and watch the film, directed by George Roy Hill, from 1969. Typing the lines here, unsaid, unheard and unwatched, would be rather like picking over bones. It would be acquisitive. I'm not going to try and conjure up that film without the right kind of agreement, either, and that kind of agreement is not simply a question of *rights*. If this idea interests you, have a read of Derrida's *Spectres of Marx*. Somewhere towards the end of the first section he has a lot to say about *conjuring*. It would be more straightforward, perhaps, if I could write characters like Haruki Murakami does, who know more about what they are listening to or watching than sometimes feels natural.

SIMON
You remember what they said?

LOUISE
I've watched it a dozen times. After Kate disappeared I kept going back, thinking she'd be there, waiting for me.

They lay there, looking. I remember all the desert and rock. I remember the dust from the horses' hooves.

Butch and Sundance leave their horse behind and climb to the top of the mountain, breathing hard, the posse chasing below, still coming. They scramble down the other side of the mountain, losing their hats, scrambling to their feet, the two of them.

We're a hundred, two hundred feet above them, looking down at them, trapped, on a ledge, staring at the narrow, foaming river thrashing through the pass below them. They go back and make themselves flat against the wall.

The posse takes position.

Sundance loads his gun, looks around him like an animal. I'm Sundance, Kate's Butch.

Butch takes his jacket off.

They argue.

Sundance looks anxious.

There are Robert Redford's eyes, always looking up if he can.

And then that look of his, the thing he does to Paul Newman, embarrassed, angry. Almost dead and he's afraid he can't swim.

Butch laughs.

Sundance looks down now, thinking about it. And they grab the gun belt together and start to shout, and run together to the edge, and they jump. There they are, down in the water, safe. They've escaped.

I look around to smile at Kate and she's gone.

*

I lose my patience, pull the headphones off and stuff them and the Walkman back in my bag. What am I doing here? I go back down to reception, past room after room with its door wedged open. I spy inside; they're all neat, each very similar. All empty.

Mr Smith is polishing a piece of silver, a vase.

'Any ideas how I can relax?' I ask him.

He sighs. 'I thought you were the expert. Don't you want to ask us any questions?'

I shake my head without really thinking about it. What could either of them say that I haven't heard already?

He looks let down. 'There're some books in the lounge. Some local history, that kind of thing.'

I nod and thank him.

'The chap who owned the place before us built up a little library. History's my thing, you know. It's a very interesting little collection.'

'So you know all about this place?'

'A fair bit, yes. But, you know, this is the kind of place that holds on to its secrets.'

'How do you mean?'

'It's rather interesting, actually.' He puts the vase down. 'When the chap who last owned the place died, it seems likely he'd been living up here on his own for years. Little old Italian chap with his books. Didn't speak to anybody, drove into town for his groceries once a week and then drove home. He turned the place into a hotel in the Sixties, then there was some kind of tragedy. One of the guests died and things ...' he hesitated. '... went sour.'

'*Sour?*'

'I don't know what else to call it. I mean, people do die in hotels. They do it all of the time. My wife and I, this is the sixth place we've had and I imagine there have been a dozen deaths. Two suicides, both pills. Heart attack. One old boy went in his sleep. Naturally you don't make a meal of it. Well, whatever happened here, all those years ago, it did for the business. Damn well hope this business doesn't do the same for us.

'The chap who owned the place, he bedded in on his own, no guests. Everybody forgot about him. The villa was in a rough old state when we took it over – and we never met him. He was dead, dead and buried, well before we even saw the advert for it. And so who is there to ask about the Villa? You go to Camaiore and people barely know it exists – *oh, that old place up on the hill. Yes, something funny happened there a long while back. Probably haunted.* You know? That sort of thing. Now,' he frowned, 'with all of this happening. That couple. At least she disappeared in town. And the murders.' He shrugs, picks up the vase and begins to polish it again.

'It's bad luck,' I say.

He nods and sighs. I leave him to his cleaning and go into the lounge, a frigid kind of a place which at least has some books. I think about Kate in here with Semproni. I look at where they sat and imagine what that was like for her. Unreal, maybe? Unreal, up here in the Villa, looking over the valley.

I cast my eye over the top shelf of books. Lots of titles in Italian. Pretty publishers' logos. I take some down, one after the other, and glance at the illustrations. Nothing seems to catch my eye, although I'm not looking for anything in particular. I scan the next shelf.

In the middle there's a blue book. I didn't notice it at first. Something makes it stand out. On the spine's a single gold letter: *K*. My hand goes stiff, as if it's made out of paper. I force my fingers to move, tugging it out. And then I hold it: something precious, as light as air, like gold-leaf, fragile and delicate as a little creature.

I open it – and a sheet of paper flutters to the floor. I see it by my feet: a few lines of writing and a signature on some pale-blue note paper. I pick it up and read it a few times. The paper's delicate; I hold it carefully, feeling my excitement grow. It's signed: John. But all there is on the page – it's the end of Robert Browning's poem, *Childe Roland to the Dark Tower Came.*

> *There they stood, ranged along the hill-sides, met*
> *To view the last of me, a living frame*
> *For one more picture! in a sheet of flame*
> *I saw them and I knew them all. And yet*
> *Dauntless the slug-horn to my lips I set,*
> *And blew 'Childe Roland to the Dark Tower came.'*

Your love,

John.

I look on the other side: nothing. I turn to the title page of the book and see Kate's name: *Kate France*. I shake it. Where's the rest of the letter? *France*. It had to be the one Louise told me about – the one Semproni had wanted. The one Kate found on her pillow. Where was the rest of it?

And what am I going to do with it? I fold what I have of the letter once, put it in my wallet and slip it in my back pocket.

Suddenly I feel the villa's emptiness: the forlorn intensity of all its empty rooms and open doors. I put the copy of *K* back in its place on the shelf, go to reception, tell Mr Smith I need to go, call for a cab and an hour later I'm on the road back to Camaiore. The same driver, the same constant speed and dramatic turns. This time I'm ready for them, though. This time I welcome them.

Mr Smith looks sad to see me go, but I think he knows it was inevitable.

CHAPTER 17
CAMAIORE, 1986

It doesn't take me long to find the hotel. I remember the street and am halfway down it, wondering what to do with the letter in my back pocket, when I notice something shifting over my head. I look up: there's a black scarf hanging out of a window three floors up. I walk into the middle of the road and see the window's been closed on it, trapping it there.

There isn't any wind, so it hangs down limply. Every now and again it shifts, like a streamer, fluttering a little. Maybe it's the warm air rising; it's hot enough. I imagine for a moment someone holding the other end and dangling it there, like you might a piece of string for a cat.

And maybe the scarf has nothing to do with me.

But I know it's for me.

I'm here. I look around and, sure enough, I see the name of the hotel the woman from the café had mentioned. I can still feel the echo of her heart from when she let me feel it. I go inside, palms itching, wondering what to do next. The old woman at reception smiles at me kindly, as if she's running a sub-post office in the country and she's just finished arranging jars of sweets on the counter.

'Dr Katiwa?'

I nod, trying not to look surprised. 'Yes?'

There's a moment where she seems to be checking something, something at the back of her mind. In the silence I notice all the keys to the rooms are on their hooks on the wall, the same as at the Villa Inghilterra. Camaiore's turning into a ghost town.

'You're here to see the ladies in room eleven?'

I feel myself blush.

There's no key hanging on the lock to room eleven. I'd missed that lonely hook, shining knowingly, all brass.

She stands back from the desk and nods. I don't know what to do. She's still smiling, nicely, generously, in a way that seems very out of place. It feels as if she's looking at me like I'm a child.

What am I supposed to say? I don't even know the name of the people I'm visiting. Well – one of them, I do. Asha.

'They're in room eleven.'

'Thank you.'

'Up the stairs, through the double doors and go all the way to the end of the corridor.'

I follow her directions, barely aware of what I'm doing, tripping on a rug at the top of the stairs, pushing so hard on the door to the corridor that it flies back, banging against the wall. The corridor's soft pink, vaulted at the ceiling. I feel as though I'm walking along the inside of a limb: an outstretched arm, or a leg. No, more of an arm. There are white doors with dark handles. I'm blundering: I'm trusting.

This is stupid, reckless, crazy and hardly happening; but it's ... what is it?

Fun?

I want to laugh. I can't catch my breath. No – there. I want to run away. I keep going and it feels hotter – stifling here in this long, little corridor. This arm.

And I'm at the door at the end, one with a crystal handle. I knock.

'Christopher?'

The voice on the other side sounds far away.

'Yes.'

'Come in.' It sounds far, far, away.

I grip the handle. It's cold, like a jewel you'd find at the bottom of the sea, or maybe some kind of a crystal shell. It's almost slippery and it turns sweetly, a movement all of its own. I push gently and the door swings inwards. I'm on the threshold of what feels like a cave. A dark room, very dark but for a menorah on a table in the middle of it, seven tall candles lighting the space, flickering, alive as if I'm in a dream.

I put down my bag. I can't see anybody, only the candles and shadows reaching around them to the room's dark edges – so dark there might be no edges. Can I make out the rectangle of a picture? The drape of a curtain? Maybe. I can't be sure.

The candles gutter and burn brighter, revealing more. There's a bed on the other side of them: a large bed with white sheets; furs piled high on it. There's a movement beside the bed. A pair of eyes peer at me out of the darkness.

'Christopher?'

My eyes slowly adjust. The woman with the heart sits cross-legged, wrapped in a black fur on an old wooden rocking chair.

'Would you like a fur for yourself? We like to keep warm,' she says.

A fur? 'I'm warm enough already.'

I think she's about to laugh but she looks serious, even puzzled. 'Asha would like you to get into bed and so, perhaps, might I. What would *you* like to do?'

I can't answer.

She draws the fur around her. How can she stand it? I'm sweating. I can feel it in the small of my back; around my neck; moisture dripping from my eyebrows.

'What would you like?' she asks.

The candles gutter again and I see Asha smiling at me from under the furs on the bed. She lifts the fur from her shoulders, allowing it to fall behind her. The scarf that hung from the window is wrapped around her neck. 'I'm hot,' she says, taking it off, speaking for the first time. Her voice is gentle, but confusing; it's in my ears before I see her lips move. There's something about the way she's talking: not her mouth but her throat.

'Are you noticing my throat?'

'Yes.'

'I don't say much. Sometimes it's hard for me to speak at all.'

I ask her why.

'People sometimes hear me, but they don't notice my throat, so they hear me all wrong. They get confused and that's hard. I can't speak to people who can't listen.' She sighs. 'Please, come to bed with me.'

She's wearing a necklace that glitters in the light: a book on a chain. The same as in the picture at the villa – the same as ... who?

'It's my story,' she says.

'Your story?'

'The one I am discovering, being here with you. It's the tale of the two of us.'

I don't understand. 'Were you both on the train?' I ask.

'On the train?' She looks sad. 'Come to bed,' she says.

I think about asking again – but do I really care? I undress and stand beside the table with the menorah. I ask the woman sitting in the rocking chair her name.

'You've forgotten already?'

'I don't know if I knew it in the first place.'

She smiles. 'You don't want to go remembering everybody's name, do you? You don't go noticing everything. But you noticed my heart and you noticed Asha's throat. I'm Josephine.'

'Josephine.'

'Yes. Like with Napoleon.'

I get into the bed and lie facing Asha. A moment later I feel Josephine behind me.

CHAPTER 18
CAMAIORE, 1986

I'm on my own, wrapped in furs.

I sit up and look around at the burned-down candles on the menorah; the light coming in through the curtains now. Then I lie still, pulling a fur over my head. I spread my fingers next to my face. It's dark and hot. I can smell sex on my fingertips, and I lick around my lips for the taste of Asha and Josephine. It felt as if I had gone right inside Asha, right down into her. When Josephine rocked on top of me, I realised her heart was like a clock.

There's a knock at the door. I don't reply. Another knock and I emerge from the covers. The door opens and the old woman I met the previous evening looks in.

'Would you like breakfast?'

'Breakfast?'

'Yes, continental or full English.' She steps inside and regards the room. 'They've settled the bill. And they paid

for an extra night, if you want to stay one more night ...?'
Her voice trails into a question.

'I don't know. May I use your phone?'

She points to a small table by the window. 'It's over there.
There would be a charge for that.'

I think of my wallet and look down at my trousers folded
on the floor. Then for my bag –

My bag.

I wrap a fur round me, jump out of bed, and hurry to the
door. The old woman steps back.

'My bag,' I say.

'Your bag?'

'I think they've taken my bag.' The tapes, I think. The
tapes and the letter are gone.

'The bag you came in with?' she asks.

'Yes.'

'Yes, they had that with them when they left.' She doesn't
sound worried. I wonder if she's dosed up on something.
'Perhaps you should call the police?'

I think about it. 'Can you give me a moment?'

'Of course.' She closes the door and walks away, slowly,
quietly, just loud enough for me to hear.

My wallet is still in the back pocket of my trousers, my
money and my credit cards untouched.

The letter. There it is – some of it. I open it up: Love, John.
John's letter. Relief rushes through me: relief I remembered
it; relief that it's there.

It's *only* my bag missing, then. Just my bag. There are the
tapes, but when am I going to need them again? I decide
to make a call, but it's not to the police. I leave, apologising.

I feel stupid.

*

I go back to the café where I met Asha and Josephine in the first place. It's empty. It doesn't even look as if there's anybody behind the bar. The door's open, though. I go inside and stand at the counter, waiting.

I know who to call about all this. First I need a coffee.

While I'm waiting, doing my best not to think about what's in my wallet, a woman, middle-aged, stout, tired and crumpled-looking in a shapeless pink cardigan shuffles in off the street in slippers; and then an old man. The old man lights a cigarette and smokes, staring into space. The woman takes a book from a pocket of her cardigan, something like my mother used to wear.

A waitress appears from an arch at the end of the bar, carrying a tray with two cups on it, rather as if she's dancing. She looks not too different from Asha; not too different from Josephine, either, when I think about it. She's tanned, with Josephine's hair and a mouth like both of them.

I watch the waitress go first to the old man, where she sweeps the tray in an arc from behind him down onto the table in front of him. He laughs. She's so graceful. She smiles and he smiles, taking her free hand in his, his one much smaller, shrunken from what it might have been. She waits until he lets go, a couple of seconds; and I think I see tears in his eyes. He says something and she bows elegantly, moving towards the table where the woman's sitting.

She serves her far more abruptly, as though she isn't comfortable with something, then she comes back to me.

I remember the letter. My bag.

She looks me over before saying a word or two in Italian.

I tell her I'm English and she nods.

'What can I do for you?'

The letter. 'Do you have a telephone I can use?'

'Over there.' She nods towards a payphone on the wall where Asha and Josephine were sitting the first time I came in.

'I'm looking for a couple of women I met in here yesterday. I don't suppose they've been here?' I describe them.

'No. Maybe they'll be back today, but, look,' she waved her arms across the room, 'people aren't exactly crawling over themselves to come here.' Her English is good. 'There's a killer on the loose. I imagine maybe they will have gone. Everyone's going. They were your friends?'

'Not exactly.'

'You look sad.'

I shrug and order a coffee, changing a note for some coins so I can use the phone.

Like I said, I wasn't going to call the police. I dial Blanca's number. It's dawn back in London, but I know she'll be up. I had learned eventually, when I at last found I couldn't make an overwhelming week do what I wanted it to – there was far too much that I wanted – that she was happy to shift her afternoon meetings to the early morning. Six, sometimes.

The phone rings.

I remember walking to the side door of her house, a little annexe where she'd made her strange, nunnish chambers, just as the sun was rising over the old church next door. I felt lonely. I always felt lonely there, walking up her drive, the crunch of the gravel like frost even in the summer. And I sometimes walked faster as I got near to the door, because, even though it felt lonely there, I sensed, really, it was the only place I could ever be sure of being listened to.

I'd ring the bell, open the heavy, black door, close it, twist an old, brass key to lock it, relax at the lock's familiar clicking into place, and then sit on an uncomfortable little chair outside her room until she opened that door, the white one I once peered through the keyhole of like a child. Sometimes I stared at the picture on the wall in that asthmatic little entrance hall with its ticking radiator, like some kind of dark, old beast, and an electric heater she seemed to ration by turning it off when she asked me to come in. Once I tried to lift the picture off the wall to see whether it was a print or a painting and then I heard her coming, scrabbled to hang it back up. I managed, just, but it was crooked and I was sure it caught her eye.

'Hello,' she'd say and smile at me, inviting me in.

I put a handful of coins into the payphone, not knowing how many I need or how long the amount I'd put inside would last. I dial the international code for England and then her number. It rings three times and she answers.

'Hello?'

'Hello Blanca. It's Chris.'

'Christopher?' She sounds distracted. She never sounds distracted.

'Is something the matter?'

'Somebody has just rung me,' she says. 'A young woman asking after you.'

'What?' I look round me as if someone had fired a gun. The waitress smiles and keeps looking, as though she realises something strange is going on.

'A young woman,' says Blanca. 'She was very friendly and said you had lost your bag, but that she had it and had found my number under "*supervisor of my many affairs*" in your little black book.'

'I'm sorry.'

'Sorry for what?'

'She stole the bag. I don't know what's going on.'

'Well, it's very simple, in one way. She obviously wants to know who you are.'

'What did you tell her?'

'Nothing. Not until she asked me a question. This was after a prolonged period of silence during which, I think, unusually, both of us were very comfortable. Is she a therapist?'

'A therapist? No, she's not.'

'A pity. I think you need to see a therapist.'

I ignore this. 'What did she want to know?'

'She asked me if you would miss your bag. At that time I had no idea she had stolen it of course, so I said, of course you would miss your bag. She seemed surprised. As if you would *not* miss your bag. So I said to her, who wouldn't miss their bag if they lost it? She said she had no idea. And she asked what I thought she should do with it. I said to take it to the police station. So, I imagine that that's where it is.'

'With the police?'

'Of course. You speak as if there's something irrational about that.'

'She stole it.'

'Well. I don't know what else to suggest. Oh, apart from for you to return to London immediately, contact one of the many excellent psychoanalytic psychotherapists I have continually recommended to you, and to continue with your work here instead of chasing sunbeams like a little dog in Italy. What have you achieved?'

For a few seconds neither of us says anything.

Then I speak. 'I'm quite sure that Louise is not responsible for either of the deaths.'

'Wonderful,' she replies. 'No shit, Sherlock. Do you feel swollen with her gratitude? Enough, at least, to get on with your life? Because, Chris, I want you to think about the fact that it seems to me you are more likely disappearing into the *navel of a dream*. Your bag has been stolen, your partnership with Simon will not survive this, and you have incurred the cost of ringing me at my most inflated rate, because, I see, it is not yet nine o'clock in the morning. That is three times my usual rate.'

'But you've never charged that much before.'

'No, I haven't,' she says. 'Acting out is an expensive business.'

'What?'

'I will leave that thought with you. Make sure you don't leave it lying around.' She chuckles to herself. 'Is there anything else?'

I think about mentioning the letter. 'No.'

'Then goodbye. No doubt I will see you soon.' The line goes dead.

The navel of a dream. What had I wanted to talk to her about anyway?

I think of a cat, Schrödinger's cat, and I feel frightened. The navel of a dream: it's Freud. The part of a dream which is unknowable. The inside of a closed box. I'm breathing more quickly. I drink my coffee and look around me: a room of desultory connections. The old man and the woman in her garment lost in their thoughts; the waitress sitting on a stool behind the bar, reading a magazine with a picture of Jackie Onassis on the front.

I buy a packet of cigarettes from her and ask for directions to the police station. She draws me a map on the back of an old till receipt.

'If your friends come, I'll ask them about the bag.'

I pause. She's pretty. But I thank her and get on my way. It isn't a long walk, but I smoke three cigarettes.

CHAPTER 19
CAMAIORE, 1986

The police station looks as though it's inside out: plain white walls on the outside. But I'm not looking at the walls when I go in. My eyes fall on the back of the woman leaning on the custody desk signing something, a policeman standing on the other side of the desk with his arms folded. Between them on the desk, as far from her as possible, stands a small tartan suitcase. He stares at her disapprovingly, like an animal glaring at a beast it doesn't enjoy being around, one that had better get out of the way quickly if it doesn't want a fight. The woman seems happy to take her time, though. The door clicks shut behind me, interrupting them.

It's Louise.

I shudder, as if I've drunk something sharp: lemon juice, cold lime.

'Chris.' She looks tired, pleased. 'Christopher?'

I smile nervously.

She glances back down at the papers in front of her and scribbles something. I guess, from the last sweeping strokes of her pen, her signature. The policeman looks at me, scanning me. He says something in Italian.

I tell him I'm English.

'You with her?'

I nod.

Louise reaches across the counter and takes hold of the suitcase. The officer places his hand on it.

'A minute.'

He picks up the piece of paper she's been writing on, turns it around and reads it as slowly and deliberately as I saw Louise write her name. He takes his hand away. 'OK.'

She thanks him as if he's held open a door for her, and he slides the case over. She lifts it down from the desk and walks across to me. 'We'd better go,' she says quickly. She's whispering.

'Wait a minute.' I ask about my bag. Nobody's handed in a bag.

'I can go!'

'You can go?'

'Yes.'

'But there's something I need to do,' I say. 'I found the letter John wrote to Kate and –'

She chucks me her suitcase before I can say any more and I take it without thinking. 'Come on,' she cries. Linking her arm through mine, she pushes open the door and hurries us out into the street.

'What's going on?'

'They've decided to let me out.'

'That's great but I –'

She tugs me on. 'Where are we going?' We're heading down the main street, back in the direction of the café I've come from.

'Anywhere. Semproni told me I shouldn't hang around. It won't take long for the press to hear.'

'Where's Semproni?'

'No idea.' She looks behind us, quickening her step. 'Back at the station. He left me at the desk with that oaf who happened to be with me when they first took me into custody. He thinks I'm guilty as hell. Coincidence meeting you here, don't you think?'

It was, but I feel as if I've been set up. I wonder who's watching us as we hurry down the street. I need to show the police the letter – but I trip, my arm slipping from Louise's, and I stumble. Her arm tightens, steadying me, a gentle anchor. We stop dead, directly under the town clock, staring at each other.

'We need to talk about this,' she says.

I let go of her arm. I imagine Blanca looking down at us. 'Where can we go to talk, then?'

'But –'

'Please.'

'I need to show someone the letter.'

'Talk to me first,' she says, 'then do whatever you want.'

I can't think of anywhere else so I take her back to the café.

*

We take a breath at the same time and stare at each other. The old man and the woman in her pink cardigan are still the only other people in the café: her halfway through her book, something with pictures of flowers, and her third coffee; him on the way to filling his ashtray.

Louise speaks first: 'You can't have the letter.'

'Why not?'

'Show it to me.'

I hesitate, then get it out of my wallet. She watches as I unfold it. 'There,' I say. 'John's letter.'

'*John's* letter?' I can't read her. She turns her face away, maybe realising I'm trying to. 'Semproni said he was letting me out because you think the same thing he does: that it wasn't me.' She stares at me, then into space. 'I didn't kill Kate or John. But if you give him the letter I'll go back to prison.' Neither of us speaks. She closes her eyes. Where's this going? Suddenly she seems to dart back into the present. 'Everything I said was true apart from what I said about the letter, the last letter, the one Kate found on her pillow.' She looks at me, we connect, but it still feels as though I'm staring into a well. I didn't know how deep it is, this well. She glances through the window. 'There,' she says, changing the subject. A man in a black leather jacket is leaning in the doorway of the building opposite, smoking. As soon as he realises we're looking at him he shifts; checks his watch. 'He's a policeman. What am I supposed to think about that? I remember him.' He looks at us, then up the street. He walks off in a hurry. 'Maybe they've only let me go so they can catch me again. God knows what they think I'm going to do. Do you think I'm going to do something?' Her lip trembles.

'No. But what are you worried about if you haven't done anything wrong?'

'If you give them the letter they'll put me back in prison.'

She's not telling me something. 'Why?'

'That's part of the letter Kate lost,' she says, touching it. She blinks as if she's hurting.

I think I understand: 'You know where the rest of it is.'

She lowers her head. I hear her breathing. 'After Kate disappeared I went back to the Villa. I was in the lounge and

I saw a copy of *K*. It was Kate's. But while I was reading it I heard Semproni arrive and ask for me.'

'What did you do?'

'I posted it.' She looks lost. 'At least I thought I posted it. I must have left the second page in the book. The first page,' she traces her thumb down the edge of the page in my hand, 'I stuck it in an envelope, put a stamp on and addressed it somewhere I knew nobody was going to find it.'

'Where? What did you do with it?'

'Semproni was going to arrest me. I put it the only place I could think of.' She points down the front of her shirt.

'And then?'

'And then –' she sighs. 'I dropped it in with the post at the hotel.'

I shake my head.

'They've got a little box at reception. Nobody noticed.'

She reaches into her jacket pocket and takes out a small, battered-looking pink address book. 'Here,' she says, flicking past A, B, and C, through F, slowing at J, then stopping at K. She places her finger on a name: *Krystyna*.

It doesn't mean anything to me.

'Krystyna,' she says, turning the book so I can read the address.

'Krystyna?' It's the address of the gallery in Camaiore. The empty gallery. 'Krystyna.'

'The woman John went to when he wanted something for his gallery. She's Czech, Polish. I don't know.'

Something about the confusion bothers me. 'Why her?'

She laughs. 'Because *she* is *K*.'

'Wouldn't somebody have guessed that by now?'

She shrugs. 'She doesn't spell it like that. I wrote it down after John told me. He knew, Kate knew, and they told me. Krystyna was his lover.'

The fact sinks in: it feels cold, icy. But I still don't see what difference it would make if Semproni gets the letter. I tell her.

She jumps up then sits down, a little explosion. 'It's none of his business.'

'What difference would it make?'

She touches her ear, looks towards the bar, then lights a cigarette.

I shake the page I'm holding. 'It's a love letter from a man to his wife. What's so strange about that?'

She sucks on the cigarette.

'What did the rest of it say?'

She shrugs.

'What?'

She laughs.

'What's so funny?'

'You want me to tell you what it said, or who it was from?'

'I know who it's from. He's written his bloody name at the end of it.' I'm angry. I'm loud.

She looks surprised and taps her cigarette on the ashtray, a green dish with a picture of a cat on it: a black dancing cat. Her voice sounds cracked, husky: 'I told you, I did the best job I could with the truth. If I told them what was really going on, they'd keep me locked up. Maybe in a prison, maybe in a hospital.'

'What are you talking about?'

She leans forward, touches the letter and whispers: 'It isn't from John.'

My anger's gone like steam. I look around. Even with her whispering, the place is so empty I imagine you can hear us from the bar. I ask her to wait and go to the jukebox. There are some songs by Bowie; I choose a couple quickly, going by the pictures, hardly able to think about it. Bowie in a dress, sprawling. The guitar riff, jarring, the beginning of *The Man Who Sold the World* plays as I sit down in front of her again.

She looks scared. 'I don't know what to say.'

'What did the letter say?'

'I only read the first few lines. And the end. What you've got there.'

'What did it *say*?'

'*My darling, you're here* ... after that I can't remember exactly.' She stubs out her cigarette, avoiding the cat's face.

'What do you mean, you did the best job you could with the truth?'

'I'm not making anything up.'

Something inside me feels as if it's leaking: a slow drip from an old pipe.

A memory forces its way forwards: my father making me shine a torch for him as he mends a pipe in a cupboard. He shouts at me: *Shine the torch. Directly!*

I breathe out, clearing my head. I need to be clear. 'I came here because of what I heard on the tapes.'

'And if you hadn't they'd probably have charged me by now and I'd be on my way to prison. But I'm not. I'm free. And I want to stay that way. *I haven't done anything.*'

Panic. 'How much of what you say on the tape is true?'

'I was as truthful as I could be to him, but I'd have told it differently to you. As it wasn't you. Semproni wanted me to speak and speak – and bloody speak – so I did. I spoke the best I could. I didn't want him to think I was mad. So I made up the stuff about John writing the letter. I never said he did it for certain.'

'What?'

'No.' She lights another cigarette. 'I couldn't ... because that letter's from Jack.'

'Jack?' Stupid. She's crazy. I get up, put the letter back in my wallet, and put some money on the table. 'I'm going to see Semproni.'

'What?'

'I'm not stupid.'

'Really?' She stands up, too. 'You wanted to know what the letter said.'

'Yeah. That's right. I think I've misjudged the situation here, that's all. I've made a complete fucking idiot of myself.'

I start for the door. She shouts: 'Why don't you read it for yourself?' I stop. 'We can go to the gallery.'

'I've already been there.'

'Then you know where it is. Let's go there. The letter will be there.'

I remember the pile of letters I found by the door.

She stubs out her cigarette. Bowie finishes singing. We are the only people in the room – the waitress has gone; the woman in her pink cardigan and the old man: both gone. I didn't even notice.

She swallows. 'And I can tell you about the letter if you really want to know.'

Guitar chords: strumming. *Rock 'N' Roll Suicide.** We stand there staring into each other's eyes.

I tell her: 'Go on, then.'

'Jack signed himself John to people he loved.'

'Jack France wrote the letter Kate found on her pillow?'

She nods.

'John's father? Jack France?'

---

* I would suggest, or would even say it's essential, that you listen to this song while reading. It's the last track on *The Rise and Fall of Ziggy Stardust and the Spiders from Mars*, released January 1972. There's a lot of Bowie in this book. We used to live under the same patch of sky.

She nods again. 'His name was John. People called him Jack. He liked it, but not when he loved someone: he thought Jack sounded hard.'

I ask, I have to ask: 'A ghost?'

She tosses her hair so a strand falls over her forehead. 'When there's a ghost right in front of you, what do you do?'

'A ghost,' I say. 'Right in front of you.' My words sound as flat as any possibly could.

'Come on, I'm asking you. What would you do if you saw a ghost? And what would you say if your best friend said she'd seen a ghost and you believed her?'

'I might not believe her.'

'Might you not?'

'No.'

'I did. Kate told me that at first, when she found the letter on the pillow the morning after the wedding and read it, and saw who had written it, she made herself believe it was from John. But she knew really who had written it. Why do you think she tore her room up looking for it? It was another letter to K. Only the K was her, Kate. The Eleventh Letter.'

'Go on,' I tell her.

'She said that she knew it was his signature and that everything before it, the whole letter, the poem at the end, it could only be from him.'

Her eyes search me, looking for what I'm thinking.

'Kate spent her life reading Jack France. I think she knew what she was talking about. When she said she'd seen him *there*, in the writing, what was I supposed to say? You're mad? She wasn't mad. She told me how she had played it with John: making out she thought he'd written it. God knows what he thought. Kate knew it couldn't be from him.

Whatever John could be – and John was lovely – he was never going to be her Robert Browning any more than she could be Elizabeth Barrett. So I didn't tell the whole truth. But not so it would make any difference to what happened to Kate or John. I didn't have anything to do with Kate and John disappearing. But if I told Semproni what I told you; if I told anybody, or you took him the letter and he started asking me again ... how can I go on not telling him the truth? Sooner or later I'd have to tell him. I'm not a liar. The only thing I helped disappear was the letter. I posted the fucking thing.'

Bowie's shouting himself hoarse: *give me your hands.*

She's telling the truth. I know she is.

Final chord. Song ends.

'Come on,' I say. 'Let's go to the gallery.'

CHAPTER 20

CAMAIORE, 1986

We make our way to the gallery and stand outside the back door.

'Do you think we were followed?' she asks. She looks flushed, nervous.

I put her case down and listen for footsteps. It's after lunchtime and Camaiore's gone quiet, sleepy in the heat. If anybody was following us we'd have heard.

I place my hand on the door. It's warm; almost, I think for a moment, soft. I turn the handle and push. It opens like it did the first time I was here. This time, though, the second door's wide open and the gallery's lit by sunlight streaming through the windows – and my heart jumps.

The floor's covered in paper, like a carpet. Something's standing in the middle.

'What's that?' asks Louise.

'It's my bag.'

'What's happened here?' She walks to the middle of the room and stands in front of my bag, looking down at all of the sheets of paper on the floor. She picks one up. 'It's a letter,' she says. 'They're all letters. What about Kate's letter?' Then she seems to think of something. 'Why's your bag here?'

What am I supposed to say? 'I don't know. I told you, some people stole it.'

'Did you do this?' She scuffs her foot on the floor; sheets slide and glide around us.

'No, I didn't.'

'No?' She sounds wary.

'No, I didn't. Somebody else has been here. The people who took my bag.'

She circles my bag, staring down at it, then looks around the room.

She bends down and picks up a letter. 'It's a bill ...' she says, '... for rubbers.'

'Rubbers?'

'Erasers. That's what it says here. A few hundred thousand lire of rubbers, staples, pencils. It's a month old. Around when Kate and John disappeared.' She starts picking up pieces of paper, reading what's written on them. 'They're all from the last month. Krystyna must have been gone since then. But what about Kate's letter?'

I pick my bag up and look inside it. There's my notebook, the tapes. Everything's still there ... and there's something else. An envelope. I take it out and feel the room around me shift as if I was on a boat, below deck, and the sea outside's churning.

Louise is beside me. 'You've gone pale.'

The envelope's sliced open, a perfectly clean-edged slit. The work of a knife. I show it to her.

'That's my handwriting,' she says, staring at the envelope. 'That's the letter. What *are* you? A magician?'

'I didn't put it there. The last time I was here all of the post was in a pile over there. The people who took my bag did this.' I show her my notebook. 'Look. This is a record of everywhere I've been since I arrived in Italy. So they read this; they read about me coming here, and they came here, too.'

'Who?'

'A couple of women.'

'Two women?'

'Yes.'

'What were you doing with two women?'

'Getting robbed?'

She's more interested in the letter. 'I want to read it properly.' She takes the envelope out of my hands.

I look at her and I hear something; something breaking above the sleepy drone of the town in the distance. Something muffled, like a howl. My skin prickles. I listen. Now there's nothing apart from voices, footsteps; the sound of traffic.

Louise fingers the envelope, closing in on the letter.

I ask her: 'Did you hear that?'

'Hear what?'

'I thought I heard something. A howl.'

'Like a dog?'

'Yes, like a dog.'

'You're jumpy, that's all. I expect everybody in Camaiore's listening for the Wolf-Man today.' She takes out the letter, turns her back, goes to the corner of the room, unfolds it and reads it. Almost expressionless, maybe waiting to see how I'll respond, she hands it to me.

I take the half of the letter I have from my wallet, put it together with the one from the envelope and begin to read:

My darling, you're here. I don't know what to say and so I'll let somebody else say it.

And there's the poem, all of it, every word of Browning's *Childe Roland to the Dark Tower Came.* I read:

My first thought was, he lied in every word.

I read to the last words, the words of the title: *Childe Roland to the dark tower came.* At the bottom of the page, after a short rule drawn across the middle of the page, a line's repeated:

I shut my eyes and turn'd them on my heart.

I close my eyes.

Louise doesn't say anything.

The sounds of the town surge in on me. At once, though, I find myself in a calmer place: one that feels wide open, empty. It frightens me. I'm looking at the clock tower at the Villa. I am: I'm looking at it. The clock tower. I think of the painting Kate found on the bedroom floor at Wasing; the picture with its long strip scrubbed away. Louise says something but I'm not here ... don't hear. I open my eyes.

'What is it?' she asks.

'I saw the tower.'

'So did I.'

'Just then?'

She nods.

I believe her.

'The clock tower at the Villa,' she says.

I murmur: 'Yes.'

'We both saw it at the same time.' She takes the letter. I don't try to stop her. 'You see.' There's something else in her voice – a different tone. Something tough and believing. 'He's in the tower.'

'What do you mean?' But I know what she means.

'He's in the tower at the Villa Inghilterra.'

'You believe me then?' She doesn't sound as if she thinks I do; and for some reason I find myself drawing back from believing her – although I do. I don't want to believe her.

I feel a pain in my chest. 'You said Kate recognised it was Jack France from the writing. But most of this letter's a poem by Browning.' I feel bloody-minded, as if I want to close a door hard and fast; as if there's water coming in all around me. I'm not convinced. Not about her, far from it, but myself.

I see the paper all over the floor, and my bag, and Louise staring at the letter.

'We need to go to the tower,' she says.

'I'm going home. You can do whatever you want.'

'No, we have to go to the tower.' She grabs my arm. 'I can't leave the country, you know. Semproni can have me arrested any time he wants.'

'Maybe you should take *him* to the tower, then.' I pick my bag up and rummage in it. Nothing's gone but everything's slightly out of place: the page-marker's been removed from my notebook; the tapes are out of order – somebody's listened to them – the Walkman headphones are plugged in, the cable tangled around my bottle of *Bandit*.

'What is it?' asks Louise. 'Why don't you believe me?'

I don't reply. I close my bag.

'Chris, help me.'

'You don't need any help,' I reply. 'What do you expect to do there?

'Wait,' she says. 'Wait there.'

I walk away.

'Look,' she says, holding the letter up. 'Please, read it again.' There are tears in her eyes.

'Keep it.'

She stuffs the letter into her mouth and chews it. She swallows it. 'There.'

'Fuck you.' And I'm gone.

*

I go back to the café. My trip to Italy's over, and, as for what I'd done, it's neither here nor there. If there's anything on my mind it's the Browning poem.

My first thought was: he lied in every word.

She ate it. Jesus. Both sheets.

I drink a coffee quickly and order a whisky. It's late afternoon and I'm on my way home, back to London, so why not? I think about ringing Blanca, but what's the point? She'll only tell me to do what I'm doing anyway – again: to go home. The same thing she said this morning. I've wasted my time: maybe Louise was lying, maybe she wasn't. What difference did it make to me?

She ate the fucking letter.

I drink another whisky, and then another.

I'm the one who lied. I convinced myself I knew what I was doing. But I'm sitting here in the café, which is beginning to feel more and more dismal, as the waiter gives me one whisky after another as though he really doesn't care. Where's the dancing waitress gone?

Six o'clock. Drunk, and I'm thinking: she ate it.

I go to the bar, get halfway there, realise I've left my bag by my seat, go back and get it, make it all the way to the bar and get a newspaper, return to my seat, put my bag on the table so I don't lose sight of it and start to read.

I get distracted. Stop. Look around me.

People seem to be staring so I pull my bag towards me. Life's leaked in on me so I put up a dam. And I read, in spite of the text being in Italian. It's almost as if I can understand it – as though I'm starting to make sense of it; with the picture of a young woman on the front page, the same woman I saw on the front page of the newspaper in Pisa two days earlier, I know. I'm reading about the Wolf-Man. He scares people. People are terrified. Nobody wants to come to Camaiore.

Well, I'm here, and I'm reading Italian.

I turn the page, annoyed by everybody else being a coward, I focus on a photograph of the two young women. I work out from the caption below that they were the Wolf-Man's victims in Pisa. Those bleak expressions: passport photos, maybe? But photos of dead people always look like photos of dead people.

I peer through my fingers at the people around me, reassuring myself of what real, living faces look like. I find myself staring at eyes, lips, noses, strands of hair falling across a brow, teeth, cheekbones, make-up; and I look down at the photographs in front of me.

I turn back to the front page, to the picture of the woman on her own, wanting to know what her face shares with the women from Pisa. In her eyes, perhaps, I see something similar; or is that something in me?

I go back to the women from Pisa.

I look about, recognising nobody and nothing; nothing in those eyes, no. I can't concentrate, really, my mind's fucked up by the drink. In fact, if I close my eyes, and why not, I think everyone might disappear.

Yes, I'd like to disappear. Good on you Jack, John, Kate – I lift a glass. This one's for you. Happy birthday, wherever you are.

I stare at the women from Pisa again.

Josephine. Shit.

The one on the left looks like Josephine and the woman on the right – Asha.

Asha winks at me and smiles. Josephine speaks to me:

'Psychosis is a state where you lose touch with reality. It sounds simple unless you begin to consider what *you, lose touch* and *reality* all mean; and, oh dear, Chris, right now I imagine you might think you're mad.'

I'm drunk.

'Not that drunk,' whispers Asha.

I mumble thank you. I read the newspaper with my forehead resting on my bag and my hands on either side of my face, screening me off from the other customers. If they could see me I think I would look white. I'm cold. My head feels as if it's floating, trapped between my hands like a giant soap bubble: clean, white, weighing next to nothing.

'Chris,' begins Josephine. 'Can you still smell me?'

I can. I can smell her.

Asha says: 'Can you still taste me in your mouth?'

I blink. I try to blink but a soap bubble has no eyes. I'm eyeless. I smell my fingers, run my tongue around the inside of my mouth and, yes, I can smell them. I can taste them.

Something's happening, running ahead of me, taking on a life all of its own.

'I am going mad.'

'No, you're not,' the two women whisper back, together.

Asha speaks. 'If you can smell or taste us, then something real happened.'

'I might just be mad.' I bang my head down on my bag.

'It is unusual,' says Josephine. 'We *are* dead. The killer killed us.'

'Oh,' says Asha, as if she's forgotten. She looks desperately sad.

'It's all right,' says Josephine. 'Unless Napoleon here decides to avenge us.' She looks serious. 'Put your fingers on the page, below my face. Imagine where my breast would be. Put your fingers underneath where my breast would be, and feel my heart.'

I do as she says. The paper feels cool ... nothing – and then there's a beat.

'It's my pulse,' I say.

'No,' says Josephine, 'that's my heart. It's beating like a drum. An army marching into battle. Can you feel it?'

'Yes.'

'That's my heart. You know my heart. It's a question of that, of heart. Your heart brought you here and that's no crime. Head should never rule heart.' She shakes her head. Asha agrees. 'You think you've been listening to your head,' says Josephine, 'when you've been listening to your heart.'

I begin to cry.

'We want to help you,' says Asha.

'We want to be with you,' says Josephine.

'Keep you warm,' says Asha.

'Look after you,' says Josephine.

My shoulders begin to shake. 'You're both dead.'

'We know,' says Josephine.

'Don't we,' says Asha. 'We were murdered by the Wolf-Man, like the others.'

'Who?' I ask.

'We can't say,' says Josephine. 'The dead can't talk about the dead. Only themselves and the living.'

'Who's the Wolf-Man?' I ask.

'No, we can't say,' said Josephine.

'Why can't you?'

'We can't say. Ghosts keep secrets; we're secret machines. Don't expect us to make sense. We care but we can't say.'

'We can't say much,' says Asha.

I saw them on the train from Pisa, talking about films.

'Yes,' says Josephine. 'Terence Stamp and Pasolini. We were dead then.'

'I didn't say anything. How did you know what I was thinking?'

'I don't know,' says Asha. 'We were the women in the station.'

'Why are you here?' I ask. 'Why are you here now?'

'We're here to look after you,' says Josephine.

'To look out for you,' says Asha.

'Why?'

'Because you're a nice man. A kind man,' says Asha. She laughs.

'You think you made a mistake by being here, but the mistake is still to be made,' says Josephine.

'Yes,' says Asha. They both looked worried. 'There's something that still might happen.'

'It *might* ...' I begin –

'Excuse me, sir.'

A man's voice cuts in. I look up and see the waiter standing staring at me, his arms folded. I can't work out if he's worried or angry. He sticks his jaw out and looks around, catching the eye of the people around us. I realise he's speaking as much to them as he is to me.

'Are you all right, sir?'

'Of course.' I find myself trying to stand up. It's difficult wondering where the floor's gone.

'Perhaps you've had enough to drink?'

I look at the newspaper and see two black and white faces: the faces of the women who died in Pisa. I can't say for sure if they remind me of anybody. I get to my feet, knocking my chair over. 'I'm going to my hotel.'

In no time at all I reach the door – and there's a hand on my shoulder. I turn and find my bag thrust into my arms.

'You forgot this,' he says. 'And this.' He slaps the newspaper down on top of it.

I thank him and stagger in the direction of the hotel I spent the last night in. They said I could stay.

CHAPTER 21

CAMAIORE, 1986

I was told there was a spare bed in room eleven.

The woman at reception wouldn't understand, though, that I already had room eleven booked. It was all arranged, I told her. No it wasn't, she said. The room had been empty for a week, like the rest of the hotel. And if they hadn't very much wanted *some* business, she said, they would be more discriminating over who they had to stay.

'You're drunk,' she said.

I told her I'd spent the night before there. That she was mistaken. I described the woman who had been on duty but she said she didn't know the person I was describing.

Perhaps I'd been at another hotel, she said. There were a lot in Camaiore, all with plenty of spare rooms.

And then I woke up here, face down in the dark, lying in my clothes. It isn't quite dark. There's enough light, flickering, orange, for me to lift my head and see the fur I'm lying on is dark. Bear fur.

I sit up slowly, my head aching, and take in my surroundings. It's the room where I was last night. I'm lying on one of the same furs. The same menorah sits on the little round table, burning exactly as it did before. The only difference: I can smell whisky. It tastes like smoke in my mouth.

I lean back, confused, stretch out and lie like a star in that big bed.

As I lie there it seems to grow warmer, softer; the fur feels coarser, as if I'm lying on dry grass in the middle of the summer. I hug the air and then I smell something, a sweet, beautiful smell, like a cunt.

I'm lying on an enormous cunt.

And I move and feel the bed, the cunt, quiver as I start to get aroused. My cock grows hard and I roll over, so I'm face down and I lie there, my cheek rubbing the fur, the hair, to feel warm skin underneath. The cunt moves, trembles as I shift my weight.

Then I hear a clock ticking, and ticking more loudly.

A bell rings. An alarm bell. And more bells. It's as if every bell in the hotel is ringing.

I sit up. The bed's a bed. The bells are silent. A clock ticks softly somewhere and my attention falls on the flickering candles. I can't be sure, but they're getting brighter: brighter and brighter, as if the room's on fire. The flames aren't any bigger but the light ...

Beyond the candles, through their impossible, burning light I see the door: flat, like a screen. Then the surface seems to move. It ripples, shifts, like the surface of a pond, and a form begins to take shape in the wood, the contours of a person.

My father. My father's in the room with me.

My father, an old man, wrinkled and frail, the way I remember him days before he died. He holds up his shaking hands. They're covered in cuts. He's wearing a short-sleeved white shirt, buttoned tight over his fat stomach and I see the wounds running up his arms. He turns his face from side to side and I realise what I'd thought were wrinkles are more cuts, freshly bleeding. Blood drips down his cheeks, running onto his collar. He lowers his head: the dome of his skull is a mesh of wounds.

'Dad?' My voice shakes. 'Dad?' I want to touch him, to hug him. 'What's happened?'

He looks at me with his animal eyes. Beast-eyes. He's here in my room, eyeing me like a dog.

I remember him coming into my room when I was a boy and throwing cold water on me to wake me. I shift back so I'm supported by the wall, and I'm breathing so quietly. I don't want him to hear me breathe.

If I kept still, really still, he might not notice me. Dad. He looks so tired, so sad.

Then he's speaking to me in his broken, stupid English, as if he's spitting out words: as though no words are good enough for him, although no words were ever comfortable for him, having to speak in English.

'What is this?' he hisses. *Is* sounds *eez*. *This* sounds *theez*: '*Wot eez theez?*'

I wait a moment before I say anything. It feels as if there's a cold mist around me – something I can't see, seeping into me like gas. Pernicious, but now I know it.

Fear.

'*What* is *what*?' I've said this so many times, toe to toe, terrified but indignant in my best public school English, pissing his ignorance up the fucking wall.

'Thees.' His voice isn't deep; it grates.

'It's a hotel room. What's wrong with you?' I don't want to hug him. I'd like to crush him. 'Why are you covered in cuts?'

He shakes his head and moans. 'One cut,' he says, 'for every word I say in rage. Every fochen word. One cut for every time my tongue cut someone.' He reaches into his pocket. 'So I do not bleed,' he says, 'thees is what I have.'

He's got something in his hand: something soft and horrible. A kind of a creature, something like a bird. 'Look.' He opens his fingers. There's a doll standing on his palm. I think it's a doll until it moves and stares at me out of sad eyes. It lifts its hands, reaching for me. It's my mother. She gets down on all fours and crawls over my father's wrist, grabbing hold of his skin with her tiny fists so she doesn't fall, licking his wounds, making her way to his neck.

'She does thees so I do not bleed,' he says.

'Mum?'

'She doesn't talk. Her whole life she does not talk.' My father's expression is awful, but also almost nothing at all, like something that's been printed without any real care. A poor illustration; a weak design. 'She say to you that I love you. I do not love you. These cuts, so many of them.' He looks at his arms where my mother wriggles like a slug. 'Because of what I say to you, your mother, your brother, your sister.'

His whole life I never heard him admit to doing one thing wrong. This is my father? And that creature: that's my mother?

'Can you sit down?' I ask him.

'I can,' he says.

'Do it, then.'

He sits down in the rocking chair where Josephine sat the previous night. He lowers himself carefully and I think of all his cuts. He crosses his legs, wincing as the weight of one leg falls on the other. My mother crawls on her knees to his wrist and pats the back of his hand, a happy, dazed expression on her face that I've seen many times before. He glances at her without much of a thought, picks her up and puts her back in his pocket.

'Do you believe in me?' he asks.

'I don't know,' I answer.

'You see her? I do this to her. You hear me? What else you want?'

He gasps and places his hand on his shoulder. 'A cut. Another cut. You see what I do to be here with you? I bleed.' He puts a finger to the side of his face, draws a breath, places his hand back in his pocket, takes out my mother and drops her on his shoulder, like a parrot. She begins to lick his cheek.

'This is just in my head,' I say.

'Where else?' says my father. He rips open his shirt and shows me his chest. 'You see?' His voice is broken, hoarse. 'You want to be like me? You think you help somebody but you trap somebody *because you are so scared.*'

The words hiss out at me. I'm panting, my skin prickling. Fear.

I hear a faint, distant sobbing and realise it's my mother. So she *does* speak. She draws her hands over her face and I hear her thin, thin voice, like a whisper from behind her fingers. 'Chris,' she says. 'Chris. Look at your father. Look at me. In our lives we bound ourselves like this. What do we have in front of us? I will always be a parasite and he will always cause pain.'

I look at my mother: tiny, quiet now. I feel cold, my body starting to tighten, everything closing in around me.

'Mum?'

My fingers are spread-out, bony like a bird's claw, and they began to bend upwards, against the joints, and then down, inwards, like talons. I remember Blanca's breasts like fists. I see my mother and I want to squash her. I see my father and I want to jam her in his mouth, choking him.

The candles die.

*

Did I faint? Did I sleep? I look at my hands, my fingers, resting on my chest. I'm on my back. I turn over and stare at the menorah, the light of the candles as cold as the moon. I think about a giant harvest moon casting long blue shadows on me. I see the shadows on my hands and I shift onto my side, staring into the light. It feels mysterious, as if it's giving me something.

There's something coming.

There are shapes on the door like ripples on a pond, and they grow firmer, as if a breeze is growing stronger. But there's no wind, only the sound of a distant wind and the crackle of flames, as if a brazier stands between me and the door.

Two figures appear, bringing with them the sound of the wind. The flames gutter and the light is so strong I need to look away, but I can't and the figures come towards me, my eyes stinging.

Josephine and Asha – naked, they keep coming, through the flame: walking forwards. They are transparent, their skin a milky glow.

They stand at the end of the bed, staring at me, smiling at me, the candles behind them as clear as if the women are made out of glass. They're wearing those necklaces with books. My hands shake.

'Who are you?' I ask.

'Who were we?' asks Josephine, as much to herself as to me.

'I know your names.' My voice is full of fear again. 'But who are you?'

'We're spirits,' they say together.

'Ghosts,' says Asha, 'because somebody killed us.'

Their bodies look darker for a moment, more opaque.

'Because we're angry,' says Josephine, as if she can read my mind. She can read my mind.

'Because we are hurt,' says Asha.

'Why are you here?' I ask.

'You saw my heart,' says Josephine. 'Nobody else has.'

'We're ghosts,' says Asha. 'Nobody can see her unless they've seen her heart.' She looks at Josephine, her eyes suddenly full of tears. 'Unless they have seen my throat.'

'We're all alone and we don't know why,' says Josephine.

'And we bumped into your parents,' says Asha.

'Your mother asked us to look after you.'

'So, we have,' says Josephine.

'As far as we can.'

'My parents?'

'We're all alone, apart from other ghosts.'

'We need to show you something,' says Asha.

'Why are you doing this to me?'

'Because you can see us.'

'Don't you know why?' I ask.

Josephine touches the book on her necklace. 'A ghost wears her story without knowing why. We feel our stories and follow them. We can't read them. We can never know them.'

Asha raises her hand and touches her book. 'My story,' she says.

Josephine reaches down to me and takes my hand. To my surprise she feels warm. I look at her fingers and through them I see mine.

'Come with us,' she says, and she leads me towards the candles, to the door. For a moment I taste the wood and then – I'm standing in grey, watery daylight at the bottom of a flight of stone steps.

Josephine's on my left and Asha's on my right. There are people, mostly men in coats, all around us, everybody looking up the stairs. There's somebody standing on the stairs

'They can't see us,' says Josephine.

Cameras flash.

'Where are we?' I don't need an answer because as soon as I've said this I recognise the figure on the steps – the way she's standing. And other things make sense ... how does this make sense? The men's hats; their heavy coats. Their ties and their cameras: they're holding old-fashioned cameras.

Flash guns fire.

This is the photograph from the *Dundee Herald*. This is 1947: Maria Stein, Dad's fifteen-year old niece, looking like a child in clothes too grown-up for her: standing on her own on the courtroom steps, broad stone steps – deserted apart from her. She's awkward. A heavy tartan skirt covers her legs right down to her ankles; it's too much like a blanket. She's wearing some kind of a jacket, buttoned up, and a hat concealing her hair – a hat like a pith helmet, like a jungle soldier would wear.

Her face? That's her face: a square jaw and her lips, like a smudge, and her eyes like dark pebbles, almost as if they've been burned away. Eyes that could mean anything to anybody.

Surely the moment anyone saw Maria Stein's eyes they'd know what she was like?

'No,' says Josephine. 'Look harder.'

I look. Her eyes are the eyes of somebody who knows closing them won't do any good. She stands there with her fists clenched, her toes turned slightly inwards, her head down and her mouth closed. Maybe she's trying to remember what I know her solicitor told her: *don't let on how well you speak English; don't let them pick up on your American accent,* the one she learned from the soldiers she slept with when she was in the Allied transit camp, which made a secret of the German accent she picked up doing the same in Auschwitz, before she ended up with my father.

She's fifteen. I feel sick.

'Why are you showing me this?'

Josephine and Asha don't reply. The journalists keep taking their photographs. Maria looks and she sees me. She opens her mouth –

*

Now we're somewhere else. We're standing in a suburban hallway behind a woman who's about to answer her front door. She's looking at the figure on the other side of the frosted glass window. I can't tell much of who it is: there's dark blue; it's somebody large and Maria has her hand on the doorknob but she isn't turning it. I can hear her breathing. She says something to herself in Polish. I half understand. One of the words is a swear word.

Whoever's outside knocks again.

She opens the door. Asha and Josephine watch silently.

It's a policeman. He nods sharply, staring down the hall past Maria.

'Hello,' she says. She isn't looking at his face. There's a parcel under his arm, the string used to wrap it dangling down to his boots. She wobbles; he notices but doesn't seem interested.

'Is your uncle about?'

She shakes her head.

He scowls. 'He's not in?'

She shakes her head again. 'My uncle is away.'

'Is your auntie in?'

'My uncle is away.'

'Not your uncle. I'd like to speak to your auntie.'

'He is away.'

He raises his voice, almost shouting. 'Can I speak to your auntie? Julia?' My father's first wife.

Maria steps back. 'Yes I will get her.' She sounds terrified and hurries out of the hall. We follow her through the kitchen and out through French windows into the garden. At the end of the garden, under an apple tree, Julia, a plump, unpleasant-looking young woman sits on a bench. It must be late summer because she's surrounded by ripe fruit.

She sees Maria straight away. 'What is it?' She sounds Scottish, clipped.

Maria's muttering to herself.

'Have you done with the dusting?'

Maria shakes her head.

'Have you broken something?'

'No.'

'Then what is it?'

Maria says nothing.

Julia stands up. Her face colours and she slaps her hands together. Maria jumps. 'What is it, ye little fool?'

Still Maria doesn't reply.

Julia launches herself towards us, cursing Maria. She stops when she hears the voice booming from the front door:

'Am I gonna hae to wait here all day?'

She bustles past Maria, past us, though we follow, rushes through the kitchen, knocking a chair over, and without stopping to pick it up continues into the hall. Instead of addressing the officer standing in the door, though, she reaches for the telephone.

The sergeant's voice stops her. 'Mrs Katiwa?'

'Sergeant Knox?' She doesn't look at him. Her fingers brush the receiver. She still doesn't look at him.

The sergeant steps into the hall. 'Mrs Katiwa?' He sounds confused. He takes off his hat and waits. I understand this. Julia was the local laird's daughter. He's wondering whether he should have gone in – and he steps backwards, back out of the door.

Julia sees. She snaps: 'Did I say you could come in?' This isn't the right thing to say. Knox comes back in, scowling even harder than before.

'Mrs Katiwa, I need to speak to your husband.'

'He isn't here.'

'I can wait.'

'He won't be back today. He's working in Edinburgh.' She moves away from the phone.

'Is he contactable?'

'Not today, no. Can't it wait?'

'No, I'm afraid it can't. I need to talk to him about a very serious matter.'

Maria's crept into the kitchen and is listening, standing beside the overturned chair. Julia takes the sergeant into the immaculate front room. We go after them. She offers him one of the hard chairs by the bay window. He refuses, saying he'd rather stand.

The two of them stand in silence, the noise of the carriage clock on the mantelpiece and the sound of the sergeant's wristwatch magnified, ticking together.

The sergeant speaks first. 'I really need to talk to Mr Katiwa.'

Julia's eyes have fallen on the parcel under his arm with its dangling length of string. 'And I said he isn't here.'

'If you tell me where he is, I'll find him.'

'I'm ringing my father.'

The sergeant puts the package down on the chair Julia offered him and clears his throat. 'This came back from customs. It was sent from this address.'

Julia approaches the chair and reads the address on one side of the package. 'But that isn't my handwriting. It isn't my husband's either.'

'Then whose is it?'

Julia shouts for Maria. There's a creaking outside the door, too close. 'Maria, come inside.'

Maria comes in, red-faced, and stands in the middle of the room. Julia points to the address on the package. '*Is that* your handwriting?'

'Yes.' She begins to cry. 'The woman in the post office, she told me to write it on there.'

Julia looks at Sergeant Knox triumphantly. 'What's inside it?'

The sergeant looks uncomfortable. 'Buttons,' he says, 'buckles, medals. All silver.'

'Silver.'

'Yes, she was trying to send your silver out of the country.'

'I think your business is done now,' says Julia.

A week later Sergeant Knox was on duty when the woman from the post office came in saying Maria had come to her asking for help. Her uncle had beaten her. She showed her the bruises. Something had to be done.

*

And – I'm standing on the kerb of a street somewhere on the edge of a city at night, the concrete pillars of a raised highway in front of me, the sound of traffic at the top of them, halogen lights casting a deadening glow around us.

I realise how long it is since I've spoken. 'Where am I?'

'Duchess Drive,' says Josephine. 'Los Angeles.'

The name of the road feels important but I don't know why. I breathe in the warm night air and listen to the noise of the traffic. It sounds as if somebody's telling me to *hush*.

I look down at the curb and move my toes. I'm barefoot but the dirty stonework feels soft, as if I'm standing on a carpet.

'Does it feel good?' asks Asha.

She's looking at my toes, watching me wiggle them, and she's smiling, but still somehow sombre, as though she was smiling in a church.

'Yes,' I say. 'It doesn't feel like stone.'

I wait. She doesn't say anything else.

'Why do I feel so calm?' I ask.

'Maybe because you're with us,' says Josephine.

She squeezes my hand tighter.

We stand there with the noise of the traffic. A siren in the distance.

'Why are we here?'

Asha shakes her head. Josephine places her other hand on mine. I look up. The sky's dark, velvet, purple-black. I can see a few stars and the crescent of the moon. It looks sharp, something claw-like about it. I'm calm, but now there's something else as well, a feeling that something's going to happen. A sense of anticipation I could do without. I ask them again:

'Why are we here?'

Asha looks down at the surface of the road. Josephine gazes off to our left where Duchess Drive rises gently until the lights running along the side of it merge with those on the freeway about a mile away.

In front of us, through the pillars supporting the freeway, I see warehouses. An empty car park. Behind us it looks black, some more buildings, dotted street lights, some of them not working. A great blunt edge to the city, peeling into the darkness. It isn't ugly; it isn't beautiful. I look at my toes.

'Why are we here?' I ask.

Josephine tells me to wait. She looks into my eyes as if she's reading me, her pupils shifting across a page. 'Look,' she says, nodding to where Duchess Drive meets the freeway. 'This is the first exit out of the city.'

The hush of the traffic is broken by the noise of a lorry leaving the freeway, its headlights bearing down at us. Behind it there are two cars; in the distance, somewhere, that siren I heard earlier, like the call of a seagull against the rush of the sea. We wait as the vehicles approach us. Chrome bumpers. Tail fins. A curved bonnet on the truck like a pillow. Dirty exhaust fumes. They pass us leaving a scent of lead.

'What year is this?'

'1966,' says Asha, 'in California.'

I know what's going to happen.

A new set of headlights appears from the freeway, these ones moving more quickly, far too fast – tyres squealing. Behind them there's that siren. A second car, a police car pitches towards us, its headlights flashing. The first car keeps going, accelerating, and there's a bang, like a gunshot: one of the front tyres bursting – because I know this is what had happened.

On the 16th of June 1966, at three o'clock in the morning, Maria Stein left the freeway pursued by two LAPD officers. They didn't know who she was, or that she was a woman with no previous criminal record – although she had been involved in a major criminal case in Scotland, in the United Kingdom, some years earlier.

She was driving a stolen car. She was full of alcohol and cocaine, and barely conscious. The front near-side tyre of her car ran over a six-inch nail which they later retrieved from the tyre.

Josephine, Asha and I watch as the car slews to the left, sparks flying as the chassis grinds against the tarmac – and it rolls over, and over, the headlights go out, the sound of smashing glass rising up into the air with the siren. There's a sudden, deadly metal slap; a crunching of metal on concrete as the car hits one of the pillars supporting the freeway.

Everything seems to shake.

The police car stops. The siren stops and, once again, there's almost silence. Just the hush of the traffic above us. No flames. Nothing more violent.

'Come on,' says Asha. Josephine squeezes my hand and we're back in the hotel room, the candlelight as gentle as it can be. I sit down on the end of the bed. Asha goes over to the window. Josephine kisses my hand and lets go of it. I feel sad and cold.

'Why did you show me that?' I ask.

'It isn't for me to say,' Josephine says quietly. 'It's your past, not mine.'

'It's my father's.'

'And yours.'

Asha looks back at me. 'Your father wanted to help her,' she said, 'and that's how everything ended.'

'Like that,' says Josephine. 'Accept that you're powerless. You're not Napoleon.

The candles flicker. They're gone, both of them.

*

It's almost one o'clock in the morning, dark outside and the hotel's silent.

Which isn't to say it's quiet. I've watched fish in an aquarium and they look silent the way I feel now: mouthing their silence.

Jesus, am I so drunk I didn't realise I just woke up? I stiffen, full of panic. A dog dropped in the middle of a field, a million miles from home. Where am I? I put my fingers to my face, the fingers of both hands, and I feel myself tremble. I hold them there. Slowly, very slowly, as I allow my eyes to take in the room, and I remember the room, and getting there, the fear starts to leave me. I take a breath. I smell things. On my left hand I smell whisky and cigarettes, on the other I smell Josephine. Asha. And whisky. I remember how much I drank earlier and wonder how I can feel so clear-headed. I get up, go to the bathroom and drink out of the tap.

Ghosts?

I stare at myself in the bathroom mirror.

Ghosts?

I listen to the hum of the extractor fan. There's a small bar of soap on the edge of the sink. I wash my face and drink some more, the water soaking the neck of my shirt.

My cuffs.

Ghosts?

I'm drunk.

I got drunk, came back to the hotel room, collapsed on the bed and dreamed. I dreamed my ghosts up out of my drunkenness and now they're going, washed away.

I look at the water disappearing down the plughole.

I listen to the extractor fan and the noise of running water. I stare at the yellow light and the over-clean bathroom tiles. And I feel my hands on my face. My bare feet on the cool linoleum. These things are all real.

There's a window in the bathroom. The glass is frosted, outside blurred, but on the other side there's a light. I lift the catch and open it, pushing it open – it feels as if nobody's done that in years. The hinge grinds; warm air balloons in, so thick with the heat I can almost taste it. Warm night air. It takes me a few moments to adjust to what I'm seeing – it's some sort of courtyard full of metal ventilation shafts. Opposite me, about twenty feet away, there's another bathroom window – the same frosted glass. On the other side, the light's on, and somebody's moving in there. Washing, cleaning their teeth. It's a man: I can see his silhouette and it calms me.

I look up and see the moon shining. A thought comes to me: a familiar, consoling one. It's the same giant piece of rock I've been looking at since I first cast my eyes towards the night sky. I know I need to get out.

I'm still not quite sober – I know that much. But I need to get outside, to get the dreams right out of me, like I want to throw them up. Inside, I can still sense their vibrations, as though they are breathing. I'd like to choke them, I think. And I wonder about another drink. Maybe I can drown them.

I've had enough to drink. I need to walk them off. I have to put one foot after the other until the sun comes up. I picture my journey home in a moment: the walk to the station, the train to Pisa, the flight to Heathrow, the train to London, the tube to St Pancras, the train to Canterbury, the walk to my house and the climb up the stairs to my bed. I lie down. And I sleep.

The bathroom suddenly feels stifling. I get out of there – out of the room. I go down in the lift. The woman on reception eyes me like she knows something's going on. I nod, put the key on the desk in front of her, and keep going out onto the street: one foot after the other.

It's quiet outside. It's closer to two than one, but still the very middle of the night. I hear a few voices in the distance, nothing near. Some other sounds drifting in from the hills which could be anything: cars, a train. I set off, with nowhere in mind. I walk along the main street and pass the café where John saw Krystyna, snatching a glance at my silhouette and wondering if anybody in there's looking at me. The doors are closed. I slow. The lights are off. I stop. I turn and look inside – and I can make out the portrait of the old couple who own the place; and I realise, without quite knowing why, I have passed the church opposite.

Blanca. Something about Blanca takes me back to the church doorway. I push it. It's open. I go in. Inside it could be any time – church time lit by candles and a weak electric light. There's the little red light at the front, near the altar, the one which must never go out; it mesmerizes me.

It's cool in here. I approach the altar, aware of the sound I make passing through the building's stillness, and sit down on a pew at the front. What would Blanca say now?

I think about all of the times I turned up at her little place next to the church, with its churchy smell and walls. Her couch. Her chairs. Her room was a relative of this one, all right. A little cousin of an old Italian church like this one.

They're all over the world, I thought: churches descended from churches like this.

'Christopher?' I know it isn't her voice, just a thought of her. 'Chris,' she says. I have her in me, installed in me as much as my father or my mother. What would she say now? I never knew what she would say, but the longer I worked with her the more I had a sense of it. That didn't make any difference. I could have known almost exactly the content of what she would say, but it was the precise words that mattered. There was nothing general about Blanca. She was always aware of what a word, an exact word, might contain – even if that was beyond words. I can only remember one time, towards the end of the time we worked together, not long before she died, when what she said seemed to come out of nowhere.

'I took the train,' I remember her saying, out of the blue, 'without thinking anything of it.' We were talking about a patient of mine, a Jewish woman, and what we'd been discussing had nothing to do with trains. 'I was a little girl and I was, after all, with my mother and my father, my brother and my two sisters. I don't remember so much of the journey, just the cold, and the crowdedness. Maybe I slept. Perhaps I was ill. When we got off the train I was hungry and something distracted me. I looked very young. Somebody picked me up, it was dark and I don't remember what he looked like, but that he was a man with big, hard hands and I could smell oil, and something metal brushed against me. It would have been his gun, I imagine, slung over his shoulder. He picked me up and put me down somewhere else. I heard my mother's voice, crying out for me. A dog barked, one of the big Alsatians. It was like a wolf. A German wolf. I was so scared, all of a sudden, as if the ground was opening up. Then my mother stopped calling for me and somebody took my hand. A woman I didn't know. That was the last time I was with any of them, with my family, on the platform at that station.' As she spoke she had slowly started to close her eyes, and she looked so worn away. 'I remember the German guard with his gun, and the Alsatian. The woman who took my hand became my mother.' She opened her eyes and looked surprised. 'Why am I telling you this?'

I searched for a reason, almost as if I wanted to rescue her.

'She's Jewish,' I said. 'The woman I'm working with.'

'No,' said Blanca. 'That's not it.'

I knew it wasn't. I had worked with other Jewish patients and she had said nothing. I had worked with other people who had described the almost indescribable things which had happened to them as children, and she had remained silent. She had observed and she had listened. There, in that moment, however, she had decided for some reason to share something of her life with me without knowing why.

'It interests me,' she said. 'Why I said that.'

I felt uneasy.

'You possibly feel,' she said, 'as if you should know something.' As usual she was right. She studied my face. 'There is a feeling in you, perhaps of guilt, that you have done something wrong by not remembering what it is, the thing that might have made me share with you a scene from my childhood, an awful scene.' She nodded. 'But you can't possibly know.'

'I don't know what you mean.'

'What haunts are not the dead, but the gaps left within us by the secrets of others. Nicolas Abraham said that, a very great man. You have some idea what he may have meant by that?'

Nothing I could put into words – nothing I could say to her. She smiled. 'Good.'

'Blanca?'

'You're in touch with it as well.'

I was confused, suddenly worried. 'Please, Blanca, you're going too quickly.'

'On the contrary. We are moving at precisely the correct pace. You and I are in touch with the space inside you where there are, where there always are, the secrets of others.' She paused and I saw her eyes begin to glitter. She raised her hand and wiped them. 'There are secrets and there are secrets. They all cut deep. I think, perhaps, in the future, you will see the sense of what I am saying.'

There was a noise at the back of the church and the memory was gone. What was it, a cat? A mouse? I realised how comforting Blanca's presence could be. As the feeling of her slips away, even a mouse seems frightening. I listen – it's a mouse, scrabbling over the flagstones, scratching at something.

I think of the mice at Wasing. The picture, scratched away; and then my dream comes back to me, of my father, with his cuts and Blanca's words: they all cut deep. I feel something like a punch – a kick; something in my head and in my stomach as though the air has suddenly left the building, and everything is unbearably still, as tense as if it might rip open: a paper bag. Bang.

There's only quiet. The mouse is gone; and it's after midnight in this little Italian town I came to by mistake. I came here to rescue someone and all I got was lost, more and more.

Or am I not lost enough? I sigh, hook my arms over the back of the pew, and look up. There's the moon through one of the slit windows. I see stars through the next. Blackness through the next three. A street light through the sixth, and stars again through the seventh. Under the windows, the stations of the cross. It's all darkness through the seven on the other side.

So I get up, and I leave the cool stillness of the church, head out onto the street – and there are the dogs which followed me to Krystyna's.

They start off, creeping, glancing back. The three of us form a procession again. This time I hear them pant. We keep moving, we keep going. I keep going as though I'm on a train – and then the dogs are gone. I'm standing in an empty street on my own: a streetlight, closed shops, an open awning.

Were there any dogs? I feel dizzy – suddenly indescribably tired. It's so hot again. It's so hard to breathe in this air. I sit down on a step in a doorway and lean against the cool stone wall. A fly buzzes near my face and I swat it away. I start to close my eyes – there's a noise. I get up. I'm wide awake. What was that? Like a sniffing? Breathing? It wasn't mine. It wasn't a dog. I shake my head: I'm not the only person in town. There must be several thousand. I look at my watch. Most of them sleeping.

I head back to the hotel. The woman watches me as closely as I approach the desk as she did when I left. The key's where I put it. I take it, go to my room and head straight for the bathroom. The window's still open. The light's off, opposite. The moon has shifted out of sight. I look in the mirror and see my tired, pale face. I listen to the hum of the extractor fan and I know I'm ready to sleep. I –

'Christopher?'

A man's voice startles me – behind me, from the doorway, out of sight of the mirror. I lose my balance as I turn, cling to the shower curtain and rip it from the rail. Little plastic fastenings rain down on me as I sprawl on the floor, the curtain covering me.

I scramble up and see a middle-aged man standing in the bathroom doorway, his wild blond hair twisted and curled as if he woke up and never thought to comb it.

'You've read my letters,' he says.

I press myself against the tiles.

'Who are you?'

'Jack France,' he says. 'But you know who I am.'

I hear a ticking; the clock in the bedroom has begun to keep time again.

He comes towards me and stops. The ticking isn't in the bedroom. It's in the space between him and me.

'You need to know,' he says, his blue eyes sunken deep, deep inside his face as if he's older than anyone, but still, I can see from his hair, always a young man as well. 'You need to know.'

'What?'

He doesn't reply.

The shower has become a darkened doorway. First it looks like the doorway to Krystyna's gallery, and then I noticed a flight of stone steps in the shadows.

'Go on,' he says.

I'm too frightened.

'But you want to know what's up there.'

'Where?'

'In the tower.'

I look through the doorway. 'That isn't the tower.'

'Isn't it?'

'You're not real.'

'Am I not?'

'No.'

I close my eyes, only I realise I still see him, like a light burning in my eyes. I remember Louise describing Kate staring into the sun when she heard her honeymoon had been cancelled.

So I open my eyes, walk through the doorway, and climb the stairs to the top – each dirty old flagstone lit by flickering candlelight that gutters as I place my foot on the first step. I climb to the top, twenty-five steps, the ticking growing louder as I climb and I find myself in a small stone chamber, the mechanism of a clock in front of me. The ticking is like hands clapping: regular, a slapping. There's nowhere to go. I turn around, away from the back of the clock face, and see a sledgehammer leaning against the wall. And on the wall is a small cross marked in white paint.

The hammer is for striking the cross.

And then darkness.

CHAPTER 22
CAMAIORE, 1986

I wake the next morning and look at the clock. It says eight o'clock and my head rings, the last vibrations of an old bell sounding as I shower and dress, throwing up in between, and thinking of nothing. Everything from the night feels pushed down, squashed into a greasy grey bundle. I check out of the hotel and sit on a bench in the main square, clutching my bag to my chest, wishing I had a clean change of clothes. The ones I'm wearing smell of cigarette smoke. I smell my fingers. There's only the scent of cheap soap.

Gradually, as I sit there watching people walk by on their way to offices, to shops, the people who get up and get moving before the tourists, I feel some warmth begin to enter my body.

I go to a café and get some coffee in a polystyrene cup. I return to my bench and drink it.

I sit and I watch and I wait, determined to leave but somehow incapable of moving on.

At about nine o'clock I feel someone approaching. I'm looking at the pavement. A lot of people have walked past – but this person's approach feels different. I know they're coming for me and I'm not surprised when whoever it is sits down beside me.

'Mr Katiwa.'

It's Semproni.

'You're tired.'

'I am.'

He lights a cigarette with a match and offers me one. 'You're still here?'

'Yes, I am.' I place one of his cigarettes between my lips, not caring what I'm smoking, watching while he places a flame at the tip for me, and suck in slowly. I rather like the taste, as bitter as it is.

Neither of us speaks anything. Still smelling the match I think of his cigarette lighter sitting in my pocket.

And time passes.

My cigarette's half-gone when he speaks to me again, staring away from us, up into the leaves of a tree casting shadows across us: little soft smudges of comfort.

'You met Louise.'

'Yes I did.'

'We picked her up afterwards. She was getting a cab to the Villa.'

I remember my mother: a leech; my father bleeding. Josephine and Asha, Jack France and the steps to the top of the tower.

I open my mouth, wondering what I can say. Nothing, of course.

'We searched her.'

I realise he's been smoking twice as fast as me. He throws down his cigarette and crushes it under his shoe.

'She didn't have anything with her that wasn't with her when she left the police station.'

'You were expecting something else?'

He shrugs. 'I'm trying to catch a killer.'

'The Wolf-Man,' I say.

'That's what they call him. Anyway, she's safely out of the way and we can both go about our business.'

'Where is she?'

'At the Villa.'

'She's at the Villa?'

He nods. 'I would say, though you're of course the expert, that she has developed something of a compulsion to be there. A couple of days,' he makes a movement with his hands as if he's measuring something, 'and if she's still doing the same thing, then I will see she's taken to the hospital.'

'What's she doing up at the Villa?'

'Who knows?' He puts out his hand. I shake it. 'There's a train in half an hour,' he says. 'Ten minutes to the station from here. Maybe you can be back in London in time for dinner.' He smiles. He looks friendly enough, but there's something in what he's saying that feels like a push.

He leaves.

I don't go to the station. I mean to, and I set off in that direction, get as far as the entrance and hear the sound of a train pulling in; but as I check my wallet for the return half of the ticket that will take me back to Pisa I start looking at a taxi parked on the other side of the street.

I must have looked at it too long because ten minutes later I'm halfway to the Villa Inghilterra.

*

I pay the driver and go to reception. The door's open. I ring the bell; nobody comes. I wait and ring the bell again. Still nobody comes. I call out. No one answers. The lounge is empty.

I walk outside and find myself approaching the tower.

Louise is by the swimming pool, staring into the water. I call to her. She looks up and waves. I think she's smiling. As I approach along the steps leading down from the tower, I see she's squinting.

'So you came,' she says.

'Looks like it.'

'I knew you would.'

'Did you?'

'Yes.'

'Well, a lot's happened since then.'

'Such as what?'

'Oh,' I breathe out, 'nothing that affects you.' I change the subject. 'Where is everybody?'

'They've gone away.' She shakes her head. 'Last night was the last straw, I think. They heard a sound like a wolf in the dark.' She looks at me.

'A wolf.'

'I heard it too.'

'A wolf?'

'I went to the window, but I didn't see anything. Maybe it was a stray dog. Anyway, they locked all of the doors.'

'You aren't afraid?' My scalp was prickling.

'No, I don't think so.'

'And they've gone?'

She shrugs. 'They gave me the key.'

'But you're on your own.'

'No.' She smiles. 'You're here.' She looks around us. 'Isn't it beautiful?'

I stare across the valley at the view: groves of olives on the hillside facing us; the clear line of the horizon studded by trees. A monastery. She looks down into the swimming pool. The sun glistens on the surface apart from the area immediately in front of us, where the shadow of the tower falls. She kneels down and presses her fingers into it.

'When you do this, it feels almost as if you should be able to walk on it.' She looks at me. 'I was thinking about the shadow Kate saw in the pond, at Wasing.' She looks up at the tower. I say nothing as she runs her fingers along the place where the shadow meets the glittering line of the water.

'Look at that,' she nods at the end of the pool furthest from us and smiles. 'There's a film I love, where Brigitte Bardot's swimming in the sea. The water's just like that.' She glances towards the horizon. 'The sea's on the other side of that. If God's anything,' she says, 'God's the sea.'

She begins to unbutton her jeans. 'I hope I'm not embarrassing you. I want to have a swim.' She kicks them off. I catch a glimpse of her legs – pale, beautiful – and turn away.

'I'm going to have a look around.'

I hear her laugh. 'Will you stay?'

'Maybe.'

'Maybe.'

I can't help looking round and see her pulling her t-shirt over her head, facing away from me. She throws it down and raises her arms. I stare at her bare, beautiful back.

She dives and I take a breath.

I look away and hear the splash of her body hitting the water. A second later I heard her cry out as she breaks the surface again.

'It's lovely in here.'

I climb the steps back up to the villa, listening to the soft splash of her hands meeting the water as she swims.

'It is,' she says. 'It's beautiful.'

'Good,' I shout back. 'That's very good.'

I look up at the tower, which makes no sense at all.

If the clock was looking towards the valley, I might have seen some sense in it, but not how it is. Anyway, the face is covered.

I approach the doorway then stop a few yards away, staring at it. I've seen it before: the dusty lintel and the splintered wooden frame. The door's closed. In my dream, in my drunkenness, the door was open. I go up and place my hand on the dark, iron doorknob and turn it. I hesitate.

I hear the splashes of Louise swimming – then I push; and the door opens, its hinges squealing. I keep hold of the door. Inside it looks the same: the same as Jack France showed me in the dream.

I feel cold, weak. I don't like the smell of – what is it? Iron?

The steps rise steeply, turning to the right. On the first one there's a jar with a candle. I make a flame with Semproni's lighter, holding the door open with my foot. Then I let it go. It shuts as noisily as it opened and I start to climb, holding the jar in front of me.

The light flickers. Ahead of me it's so black.

I hear something: rasping. My breathing. I'm tight, as if something's inside me, reeling me in. I could turn round. I could go. But I keep climbing –

I climb, one step after the other, the staircase curling and ugly, and I reach the chamber at the top.

But there's nothing here. There's no clock. There's no wall with a hammer against it. There's no mark on the wall. There's a tiny oval window – low down on the wall where the mark would have been. It's the size of a face; a small face, but an adult face, with a thin wooden frame. There could have been somebody peering back at me from the other side: a face, a mannequin face, not a human face. Instead, there is only sky, looking in.

I stoop as I approach it, my candle illuminating the turret brightly enough for me to see every strand of web, every crack in the wall. The walls are blank, almost smooth, although I can't imagine the render was applied in the last hundred years. These are old walls, heavy with history. I have to stoop further. I crouch. I kneel and I'm level with the window. I put down the candle and move closer. I touch the frame, dry and cold as bones. I'm surprised: the glass looks clean enough to see through. I move closer still and feel the frame around my face: it's like a mask. The frame touches me and I almost touch the glass. I hear myself breathing and see the glass mist. I look down.

I didn't realise I was so high. The pool looks so far away, Louise swimming in it so small. The sound of my breath; the noise of her in the water. Suddenly I hear her so clearly: the splashes; she's oblivious to me – and she is closer. I blink. I can see the goosebumps on her skin. As she turns onto her back I see the outline of her breasts, the crease of her knee as she kicks.

This isn't me looking. I know – this isn't me looking.

I want to call out to her because at once I know – I know – she's in danger. Only when I shout I make a sound which isn't me, a sound which comes from outside me. It's the sound of a wolf –

And I see her stop and look about. She's scared.

I hear the squealing of the door hinges below me. I freeze. Somebody coughs. *Something* coughs. There's another sound, a crunch, a grinding, stone on stone and silence.

I tear myself from the window, knock over the candle – darkness; but I stumble, and I fall, down to the foot of the staircase. The door's open, and it's quiet.

Louise.

I run to the top of the terrace and look down at the swimming pool. I see her clothes scattered on the tiles. She's gone.

CHAPTER 23

NOW

I was with Kay, in the Langham. She faced away from me. We weren't touching. Slowly, gently, I raised my head from the pillow. The tape recorder lay between us, a light blinking, recording. I stopped it. Through the window, there was daylight. Sunlight.

I sat up and looked at the bedsheets scattered on the floor. Here I was, half a time later, back on Langham Place. What were we recording?

'Kay?' I touched her shoulder.

'Chris?' She sounded sleepy. I lifted the tape recorder out of the way and shifted closer. I put my arm around her; lay back down with my hand on her breast. She was warm. It felt safe. Nothing had happened. It was over.

'Kay?'

'Chris?'

A strand of her hair touched my face. I started to shift, but realised I didn't need to. I could barely feel it. I could barely feel her breast, either, and she was growing cold.

'Kay?' I sat up again, my skin prickling.

She turned and stared at me, saying nothing, and touched her necklace, closing her fingers around the little book. I don't know what her expression said. There was a movement around her – colour, shifting, slipping away. Gently, very slowly, like ink washing from a page, she vanished.

'Kay?'

My heart beat faster, thudding in my ears. What was I doing? I'd done this before. No – was this the same? Was this the same thing? I went to the window like a man in a dream and rubbed at the mist so I could see out. The tree on the top of the BBC building was heavy with snow. The street was empty. Kay was gone.

I found myself looking at the tape recorder. I pressed a button and it started to rewind.

*

Acknowledgements

I'd like to thank a few people for remaining real and true over the years. Sarah, Miles, Miranda, Poppy and Rose, you live your lives in ways that amaze me and I hope I never take you for granted. Jason, did I ever really meet you or were you there all along? You still appear to be, and better than ever. Mudassar, I haven't seen you for so long but you are a true friend. Mandy ... what an extraordinary ten years. I remember you shining that torch. Clare :)). Bill / Dad: you're exceptional with dreams. Tony, they said I was your son. I'm not complaining. Marsha: you're very special to me. Mum, thank you. Dad, believe it or not. Linda, maybe we could write something together. Wandy, you are extraordinary. Chrissie, I wish you lived closer. Anna, soon, perhaps. Alex, *kurva jego.* Everyone at Charter and, of course, everyone at Dodo. Sam, without you I wouldn't have a book. You're the real thing, an artist. Alex, Thom, Tomoe, Jasmine and Jess. I'm a lucky man to have your attention. All of you: thank you. This book was written to so much music over almost seven years. It wouldn't be what it is without David Bowie, and all that that entails (Tin Machine moments). Did I mention RL Stevenson? Very few ever do, but he is a guiding light, only maybe like something hovering, glowing over a swamp.

Tom Tomaszewski, Canterbury 2016

Dodo Ink would like to thank the following supporters, without whom this book would not have been possible ...

Stephen Wright
Jim Spears
Jonathan Ruppin
Jenny Bullen
The Zebra
Beulah Maud Devaney
Tessa Brechin
Duncan Proudfoot
Françoise Harvey
Marc Owen Jones
Henrik Dahl Jensen
Helen Barrell
Maris Kreizman
Shanshan Xu
Miriam Miller
Victoria Connelly
Sharon Kivland
Blair Rose
ACHUKA
Ian McMillan
Shelley Bowdler
Olivia Bays
Paddy Reynolds
Paul Flieshman
James Miller
Caroline Goldsmith
Aki Schilz
Joseph Bain
Kit Preston Be
Hilary Freeman

James Wise
Kit Caless
Fiona McGlade
Zoe Hayes
Emma Jane Unsworth
Lynda Tahri
Sarah Jones
Andrey Zagoruyko
Tristan Rogers
RP Weston
Alison Ragsdale
Robin and Alison Jones
Dan Martin and Candice Lazarus
David Meller
Chris Williams
Sarah Harkness
Amy Clarke
Andrew Cook
Kat Smith
Ben Pattison-Gordon
Wendy Morrison
Nina Allan
Marion Grace Woolley
Louise Bach
Gabriel Vogt
Rachel Darling
Dixe Wills
Virginia Klein
A J. Ashworth
Sandra James
Jon Day
Thor-Einar Henriksen
Anders Eskemyr

Jennie Gillions
Clive Morrison
Sarah Bradley
Rachel Case
Jacques Testard
Charlie Hill
Jasmin Kirkbride
Hernan Toro
Sarah Wood
Nedda Tichi
Georgina Wright
Francesca R Zerenghi
Emily Sheehan
Jane Greig
Matthew Elizabeth Bryant
Jaimie Batchan
Sofie Blombäck
Alex Herod
Ben Stern
Brendon Warren
David Hebblethwaite
Claire Laurens
Marcus Gipps
Kirstin Lamb
Alice Furse
Philip Berridge
Luke Bartholomew
Dan Coxon
Ana Fletcher
Alison Whittaker
Annabel Gaskell
Naomi Hackett
Marion Kenyon Jones

Tania Hershman
Ben Howkins
Hannah Riches
Arno Vos
Elizabeth Aaron
Susan Osborne
Geoffrey Rabe
Tamara Craiu
Cat Rushmore
Mike Scott Thomson
Helen Swain
Graham Allen
Woody
Brian
James and Paula Wilson
Natalie Marshall
Efford-Eliraz
Nigel Parker
Paul Brindley
Katie Ley
Harriet Devine
Matthew Battle
@Not_James_Brown
Anne Marie Reilly
Adam Banks
Naomi Frisby
Maccewill J.D. Yip
Faaez Samadi
Francesca Ford
Richard Sheehan
Suzanne Kavanagh
Melissa Aho
Literary Kitchen

Ben Fergusson
David Troxler
Matthew Francis
Robert W Archambault
Anonymous
T Hill
Jo Bellamy
Alex Burton-Keeble
Anthony Trevelyan
Stephen Walker
Jayne White
Joanna Robinson
Tze-Wen Chao
Cathryn Steele
Nicholas
Julie Murray (Drynan)
Leesha Gaffney and David Evans
Thomas Sheridan
Irreverence Inc.
Nick Walden
Neil McNally
Jonathan Jones
Lucy Beresford
Anthony Brown
Amanda Jennings
Jim and Celia Spears
Russell Heath
Damian Fuller
Kate Williams
Maureen Cuell
Benjamin Spears

About Dodo Ink

At Dodo Ink, we're book lovers first and foremost. From finding a great manuscript to the moment it hits the bookshop shelves, that's how we approach the publishing process at every stage: excited about giving you something we hope you'll love. Good books aren't extinct, and we want to seek out the best literary fiction to bring to you. A great story shouldn't be kept from readers because it's considered difficult to sell or can't be put in a category. When a reader falls in love with something, they tell another reader, and that reader tells another. We think that's the best way of selling a book there is.

Dodo Ink was founded by book lovers, because we believe that it's time for publishing to pull itself back from the brink of extinction and get back to basics: by finding the best literary fiction for people who love to read. Books shouldn't be thought of in terms of sales figures, and neither should you. We approach every step of the process thinking of how we would want a book to be, as a reader, and give it the attention it deserves. When you see our Dodo logo, we'd like you to think of our books as recommendations from one book lover to another. After all, aren't those the ones that we take the greatest pleasure in?

At Dodo Ink, we know that true book lovers are interested in stories regardless of genre or categorisation. That's how we think a publishing company should work, too: by giving the reader what they want to read, not what the industry thinks they should. We look for literary fiction that excites, challenges, and makes us want to share it with the world. From finding a manuscript to designing the cover, Dodo Ink books reflect our passion for reading. We hope that when you pick up one of our titles, you get the same thrill—that's the best thank you we can think of.

www.dodoink.com